Sebastian
SECRETS

JANEY ROSEN

Dear Emma
With love
Janey Rosen
x

DEDICATION

I owe a debt of gratitude to my husband for his unending patience and fortitude, without which it would have been impossible for me to dedicate so much time to writing. Also to the many Sebastian fans on Twitter, Facebook and Goodreads; each has inspired me to continue my creative journey. I love each of you.

Janey Rosen

"And now here is my secret, a very simple secret; it is only with the heart that one can see rightly, what is essential is invisible to the eye."

[Antoine de saint-exupery]

1

Closing the bedroom door, I pad over to the dressing table and select my most seductive perfume, spritzing myself from the waist down with the musky scent. Next, my new pink silk robe is removed from its hiding place in the lingerie drawer and slipped over my head. Switching off the lamp I sashay toward our marital bed knowing that I am irresistible; a lioness prowling toward her prey.

Pulling back the heavy feather duvet, I slide into bed and wait for him to devour me; one lives in hope. Patiently awaiting a response, a soft cough fails to wake him as he lies motionless, sprawled across the expanse of our bed. Sighing heavily I decide he needs a little encouragement to stir. Turning onto my side I spoon him, my hard and needy nipples rub against his back but the heavy brushed cotton of his striped, old-man pyjama top shields him from my touch. Forgoing subtlety now, I decide upon the direct approach; impatiently reaching over his hip, my fingers trace a demanding path along his flaccid manhood through his pyjama trousers, but apparently it's as benumbed as the body it belongs to. He stirs and groans, a good sign indeed as I need him awake. Leaning in to nip his earlobe, his eyelids flutter open to my seductive smirk crafted from glossy lips. For a moment he focuses on his wife, my panted breaths breezing over his cheek. Raising a palm, the signs are promising until he swats my hand away with an irritated huff.

Humiliated and rejected once more, I wriggle away from him to the sanctuary of my own side of the bed and lie there in the darkness as I do every night, reflecting upon seventeen long years of frigidity. Tears fall unbidden, moistening my cheeks as I seek solace from my own expert fingers. The orgasm brings a release but not fulfilment and the hatred I feel for my unresponsive husband deepens, frustration burning anew within.

An incessant buzzing heralds the start of another day. Hitting the mute button on the alarm clock, I reach across to prod Alan awake, swinging my legs out of bed. It is time to prepare the children's breakfast or we will surely all be late again.

Motherhood is a gift that I thank God for every day. Conception was nothing short of miraculous as Alan's libido has always been in his boots. My ticking hormonal clock had led me to become a devious trickster and turning my cap inside out after rare sex eventually rewarded me with a positive pregnancy test and, nine months later, my daughter.

Joe's arrival coincided with the end of my frugal and sporadic sex life. He began his embryonic life thanks to two bottles of

Chablis one New Years' Eve when Alan was too inebriated to remember birth control.

Sighing at my slumbering lump of a spouse, I can't help but to wonder why we married. My libido has always been high but having notched up an indecent number of boyfriends by the age of twenty-two, I was ready to settle down when I met Alan at a friend's wedding.

Now I find myself, seventeen years on, living in a respectable three bedroom semi-detached house in a respectable village in Dorset, with a respectable job running my own business, but with a far from respectable secret. The secret brings a wicked smile to my lips this morning.

Retrieving the newly purchased tight, black pencil skirt and red silk blouse, both hidden at the back of the wardrobe nestled between winter coats, I quickly dress. Pulling up my sheer black hold-ups I savour the sensuality of the seven-denier hose then slip my feet into new high-heeled black patent shoes. *Professional, with a hint of slutty - perfect.*

A cursory glance toward the bed reassures me that Alan is still dozing but just in case, I pull on a long cardigan and button it over my exposed décolletage.

"Looking a bit dolled up for Monday morning at the office aren't you?" Alan sneers as I smooth down my skirt and check my appearance in the full-length mirror in our bedroom. *Damn, he's noticed. The one time he takes any notice of my attire is the one morning I'm dressed like this.*

"Yes well some of us like to make an effort with our appearance." My reply is venomous but in my opinion, deserved. Alan grunts something inaudible in response before heaving his overweight form out of bed and shrugging on his comfortable grey suit with boring white shirt and navy tie, as he does every week day morning. No shower. No wash. He disgusts me and I despise myself for feeling this way.

The kids are still eating their toast as I hurry them to the car, yelling a perfunctory 'goodbye, have a good day' to Alan. We are late again, which means Joe will once more lose his morning break as punishment for a lateness for which he was not responsible. I make a mental note to call his year head and apologise. As we sit, nose to bumper in the morning rush hour traffic, I reflect solemnly on the juggling act that is my life. I am mother, wife and employer – all things to many but nothing to myself. That's why my secret is so special - it is the first thing I have done for *me* and me alone; today I welcome my alter ego Elizabeth Dove, harlot and vamp. A shiver of anticipation pushes aside the guilt that pricks my conscience. *He's pushed you to this, Beth. It's not your fault.*

After dropping Joe at his junior school and Bella at secondary school, I drive to work on autopilot. My thoughts are consumed with a recurring fantasy of a strong virile man dressed in uniform, pinning me hard against a wall and fucking me until I beg him to stop … screaming as the strongest, much longed for, powerful orgasm rips through my soul. I run a red light and narrowly miss a real life encounter with a man in uniform but thankfully the traffic officer is busy issuing a ticket to a youth in a black Mazda. *Crap. Concentrate.*

The morning passes quickly as I endeavour to clear a small mountain of paperwork before lunchtime. By eleven thirty my work is done. Closing my office door, I pick up my coffee and take it to the old saggy couch where I curl my legs under me and get comfortable. I wake up my laptop and sip my coffee, drawn in once again to the forbidden world of uniform dating.

A secret fantasy about strong men overpowering me is one that has long been harboured. I've kept it to myself shamefully – it's not the sort of thing one speaks about in today's world of women's liberation and equality, even with girlfriends. When I watch movies in which a woman is arrested, I find myself imagining it's me and in my mind I always resist arrest, wanting to feel the bite of handcuffs and powerful arms restraining me. I can't even blame these feelings on my childhood, my father was lenient with me – overly so. My first recollection of this perversity was aged nine. I recall a game I forced my best friends to play in which Abigail Forrester had to be the teacher, David Seaford the headmaster and I the errant and badly behaved pupil. Abigail, Miss Forrester, always had to send me sulkily to Mr Seaford where he would have to cane my bare bottom using my pink horse-riding crop. Sometimes I left it at the stables after my weekly riding lesson, in which case Sir would use my plimsole. My punishment invariably stung but I liked it, and I liked the tingle I felt 'down there'. Abigail and David were always rewarded for playing the game – usually with 'Hubba-Bubba' bubble-gum or 'Gobstoppers' I'd bought with my pocket money. One day Abigail said she didn't want to play the game any more so I broke friends with her. David, however, said he liked to play the game but he wanted me to punish him for a change. I tried, but hated it and, soon after, broke friends with David too.

Now, in adulthood, and with a failing and unsatisfying marriage, and plethora of women's literary offerings on the subject, I'm insatiably curious to explore this hidden side of my persona.

When I enter my password and log in, I'm thrilled that my profile has been viewed by no less than twenty uniformed Gods since I last logged in. Admittedly when I check their profiles in return, most are either ugly or doppelgangers of Hannibal Lecter. One candidate catches my attention and I send him a wink. Simon, aged thirty-eight, six feet two of testosterone packaged up in fire fighter gift-wrapping. *Delicious.* I save his profile and hope to receive a wink in return.

I check my messages and feel a warm glow between my legs as I read a new message from Prison Guard John.

Babe, I'm so hard just thinking about meeting you today. Don't be late or I will

take you over my knee, and spank your arse so hard, young lady, and I won't care that we'll be in the middle of the bookstore. See you by Starbucks. Remember no panties. I want you wet and ready for me. John xxx

I grind myself down on to my heels beneath me as I read. The excitement is indescribable. I've only been a member of the uniform dating site for three days and already I have a date with John who works as a prison guard, if his profile is true. I suggested we meet today at one o'clock in the bookstore in the Blue Tide Shopping Centre. It's not too far from where we live, but a respectable and unlikely place to be spotted and a safe meeting point in case John is, in fact, a psychopath.

I know this liaison would shock my best friend Ruth Evershaw who, as a die-hard feminist, is unlikely to approve of my scheduled illicit encounter with a dominant stranger.

Reading John's message again, I can barely endure the anticipation.

Poised to reply to the message, a knock on my office door tears me away from my laptop and back to reality. Ruth's mess of auburn curls appears in the doorway. She is not only my best friend but is also my business partner. Together we run Evershaw Dove Recruitment, a personnel recruitment agency in the south of England. I love our business although it is a constant source of stress and has been since we founded the business six years ago. Ruth and I have invested a considerable amount of both time and money and are now at a crossroad, whereby the business must expand or risk being succeeded by the larger players.

"Hey gorgeous," I smile up at her.

"You've got your nose in that computer again!" observes Ruth, eyebrow raised. "You are up to no good Mrs. Dove, I know that look." My smile is one of pure innocence as she begins to pace while observing me.

"Wow, what are you wearing? You look amazing."

"Oh, this old thing? I threw it on in a rush this morning," I lie, thankful for the discretion afforded by the cardigan.

She eyes me approvingly and then raises her eyebrow almost to her hairline. "If I didn't know you better, I would say you have a date."

I blush at her intuition, which serves to reinforce her suspicion. Her eyes narrow accusingly.

"Oh my God!" she exclaims. "You *do* have a date."

"Not a date, Ruth, I'm a married woman. I'm having lunch with a friend. Sorry to disappoint, I know how you love to gossip," I tease. *If only you knew the truth.*

A deep crimson now, I put away my laptop, it's too late to email John anyway - he will be on his way to our rendezvous. I rise casually from the couch and remove my coat from the hook by the door. Powering down my desktop computer, I inform Ruth that her abhorrent suggestion is offensive and wrong.

Clearly she knows otherwise but leaves my office with a withering look, which serves only to heighten the guilt, which has settled in my core.

I have time to drive carefully to the rendezvous and to try and catch a glimpse of Prison Guard John before he sees me. That way, I figure, I can bail if he looks remotely homicidal. *I'm so nervous. What if someone sees me? How will I explain this to Alan?*

Five minutes past one. My hands and knees are trembling with fear and expectancy as I lean against the wall adjacent to the entrance of the in-store Starbucks. I am without panties and, as instructed, wet with anticipation.

The bookstore is surprisingly busy and I'm frantically scanning faces. My line of sight is set above six foot. Prison Guard John's profile stated he stands six foot, one inch. The one small photograph on the site personified impeccable affair material with a tousled mop of dark hair and chiselled features.

Feeling a vice like grip on my arm I look up. Then look down. There, standing at least ten inches below my line of sight is a receding mop of sandy coloured hair exaggerating an already too high forehead. My guilty pleasure has become my secret nightmare.

"Babe. You look even better than your pic. Come here and give Johnny a kiss." He rocks up onto tiptoes and plants a wet, firm kiss on my lips before I am able to turn my cheek to him. At five feet, ten inches I tower above the man and my ardour fizzles away instantaneously. *How the hell do I get myself out of this situation? Think quickly, Beth.*

"I'm… err, sorry you must have the wrong person." I stutter, blushing hotly. "I'm waiting for my husband." It's lame and transparent, but self-preservation and humiliation extinguish any care I have about the man's feelings.

"It's Rosie, isn't it?" The pseudonym I

created for my illicit profile. The one sensible thing I did was not to put my real name online and I am thankful for that now.

"No, I'm… Tracy. I have one of those faces that looks like everyone else's, easily done, don't worry." I say less than convincingly.

"Oh bugger. Ok, sorry about that. You sure do look like the bird I'm meant to be meeting. Nice kiss by the way! See ya."

The dejected little man ambles in to Starbucks in the futile search of Rosie.

"Yeh right. 'See ya' in your dreams. Little twerp," I mumble while making a hasty exit through the store utterly devastated.

Back at the office, Ruth is in a meeting enabling me to slip dejectedly back, in to my safe space undisturbed. I close the door and fire up my laptop, calling up the uniform dating web page and logging in to my profile, hastily deleting John. I'm about to delete my profile when I notice a message from Firefighter69. Reluctantly I open the message.

Rosie, you winked at me. I know what you want and I can give it to you. You need a strong, dominant man who takes the lead in bed. I am your man. You are my woman. Message me back. Si x

My alter ego perks up but my inner conscience screams "*delete.*" Unfortunately my inner conscience is no match for my alter ego and so begins the next chapter in my illicit journey.

By five o'clock I have revelled in a sordid dialogue with fire fighter Simon, spanning instant messages and mobile phone; all notions of my security disregarded. Having seen a photograph of Simon in his fire fighter uniform at least I know he genuinely is attractive. Not necessarily my type, with boyish good looks, but definitely most shaggable. I now look forward with eager anticipation to a sexual encounter with him on Thursday at one o'clock at the Value Inn near Bristol. The eroticism of meeting for sex is unbearable, the ache in my groin is longing for remedy, never having felt so desperate for sexual gratification in my entire life - perhaps because my body knows it lies just three short days away.

I'm restless. The children are home thanks to my mother who often collects Joe from school for me, Bella takes the bus. Alan will be arriving home with fast food for himself and the children, as is our custom on a Monday night so I have no rush to get home.

Ruth insists I go with her for an after work drink at our favourite pub, The Crooked Man. I know that my dear friend will subject me to an interrogation about my mysterious lunch appointment but nothing can dampen my spirits. *I'm wanted and desired by a real man for the first time in years and it feels incredible!*

Retrieving my coat from the back of my chair, I wrap a warm grey scarf around my neck and together we leave the office and walk across the road to the pub. Our favourite corner table is available, and Ruth sits down while I go to the bar to order our drinks. I join Ruth at our table, carefully placing the glasses on the mats provided, unwrap my scarf and, removing my coat, we enjoy the warmth of the smouldering log fire next to us.

"Ok, I want to know exactly what you've been up to, lady." Insists Ruth. "Blow by blow – no pun intended." She cocks her eyebrow in a way that implies only the full truth will suffice.

"Not much to tell" I say. "I went to meet a friend but they stood me up." Ruth rolls her eyes in disbelief, a cynical smirk playing across her lips.

"Jesus, Ruth. What kind of woman do you think I am?" I say with a mischievous glint in my eye.

She is not buying my story so I divert the conversation to sex, in the hope that I shock her into distraction. "Here's one for you. Have you heard of vanilla sex?" I ask.

"Christ Beth!" splutters Ruth, choking on her Bacardi and coke. "I'm not that naive. It's where the man smears ice cream on the woman. The things you come out with!"

I love Ruth, she always thinks she knows it all and is disgruntled when proven otherwise. Shaking my head at her ignorance, she rolls her eyes once more. "Vanilla sex," I inform her, "is straight boring sex whereas did you know, some men like to dominate women and tie them up!" I just want to gauge her reaction, not to give her too much information.

Ruth's eyes widen, as I know they would, I so love to be controversial. Ruth can't resist then giving me a lecture about how I'm setting women back one hundred years by even paying lip service to such matters. I declare that what happens between consenting adults, is perfectly acceptable, and a lively debate ensues for the next ten minutes.

"What's this all about Beth love? Is everything alright with you and Alan?" Ruth sits forward in her chair, her hand resting on my knee, a look of anxiety apparent on her face.

"I want *more* Ruth. I'm just so tired of my life. I know I've lots to be grateful for - Alan, the house, healthy kids, good job. I just want more."

"We all feel like that sometimes, Beth. It's your age. You're nearly forty, the hormones are rampant and it makes us feel dissatisfied. Honestly, there are many worse off than you."

My friend is well intentioned but her words do not temper the emptiness I feel. Ruth has been divorced from Ed for four years and lives contentedly alone. She lives for her work and never seems to complain about her lot, nor does she seem lonely. I envy her peace of mind.

"I want to feel needed. *Wanted*. To meet someone who will command me and protect me. Make decisions for me, and not put up with my crap. I want hot torrid sex, Ruth. I am sick of sharing a bed with a man who abhors touching me. I've been thinking about leaving Alan."

Ruth is shocked. "I had no idea things were that bad," she says anxiously.

"Have been for years Ruth. I just don't talk about it. I just presumed it was *me*. But, the more I look into it I see that other couples don't live like us. It's not normal, Ruth. He's not normal. I want what other people have."

"It's a fallacy." Ruth retorts. "All marriages are the same eventually. It's all sex and candles until children come along and then couples settle down. Just buy yourself a raunchy book, a new vibrator and fantasise, girl."

"That's just it Ruth. I'm not prepared to settle for that any more. I'm nearly forty, if I don't change my life now, no man will want me. My clock is ticking Ruth. Wrinkles are appearing every day and before long I'll be too arthritic or senile to recognize a cock, let alone be able to do anything with it." We both break into a laughing fit and it is cathartic.

It's been a long and tiring day and as I pull

into the drive of our neat suburban house, I'm looking forward to an early night with my book and a glass of red wine. Alan, as usual, is sitting in his favourite chair in front of the television watching a sci-fi documentary he has recorded on the TV hard drive. Our evening together looks set to continue it's usual routine. I'll put Joe to bed, Bella will grudgingly do her homework and then disappear to her room for the evening to chat online with her friends. Alan and I will barely talk. He will retire to bed at ten o'clock and leave me working on my iPad or watching television. He will be comatose when I turn in and I will lie awake until the early hours of the morning, feeling frustrated and bitter. No sex. I do wonder, night after night, if I'm *so* unattractive and undesirable that even Alan, who's no Adonis, doesn't want me. *Simon wants me and soon he'll have me*, I remind myself.

My regular source of orgasmic satisfaction is provided by the contents of my hidden toy box. My favoured toy of the moment is my neon pink Rampant Rabbit. With seven functions it is apparently "perfect for the rampant connoisseur!" I guess that describes me. It does make me feel seedy using my toys in private but a girl has needs. Usually my rabbit accompanies me to the toilet, as that is the only room in which I have privacy. Recently I treated myself to a tiny vibrator the size and shape of a lipstick and this has perked up many a boring day at the office.

Alan and I have had many arguments about sex. I would never divulge to anyone, even Ruth, that we've only made love three times in five years. I think it must be me - I must be detestable. *Simon doesn't think so.*

My self-esteem is at its lowest ebb despite constant reassurance from my mother and others that I'm an attractive woman; tall with long wavy blonde hair and, although I have the remnants of a baby belly I'm not otherwise overweight. I consider my facial features to be acceptable and unlikely to turn milk sour, and I receive compliments on my cornflower blue eyes. Yet clearly there is something lacking in my persona, which would otherwise make me desirable.

I've pleaded with Alan to agree to counselling or sex therapy sessions but he says that he won't discuss our private business with strangers. He says 'he is who he is' and tells me that all married couples are the same. He blames my literary choices and movies for putting unrealistic ideas in my head. "Those books you read and films you watch are pure fantasy," he rebukes. I disagree. My books are indeed my escape but I deeply yearn for everything I read to happen to me. I know that not all couples are like Alan and I. This is why I began looking at the Internet late at night and at work, I know that web sites exist, solely centred on pleasure. Uniform Dating is only one such site, I have visited others and am becoming increasingly curious about BDSM. This is truly tapping into the darker side of my persona and I only browse those pages after a glass or two of wine, when my inhibitions are lessened. *Oh why can't it be me receiving the lashing from the leather belt?*

"Have you had a good day?" I ask, sitting down with a large glass of Claret, having settled Joe in bed and helped him with his homework.

"Same as usual. You?" He sips whisky from his favourite tumbler, not averting his eyes from the television as he talks to me.

"Same as usual. What take-away did you get?"

"Burger and chips. I was going to get Chinese but I noticed last time they've put their prices up – bloody ten pence on the rice. Can you believe that?"

Ten pence? Who cares, you tight sod? "Daylight robbery if you ask me," I reply caustically. "How was work today?" I try to kindle the conversation, partly through guilt at my attempted infidelity today. Alan has worked for the same company, Best Business Solutions, for approaching twenty years showing no ambition, nor desire for promotion, instead he says he is happy to have a secure job in today's volatile workplace. This conjecture would be credible if he didn't always complain about his job and colleagues. IT, he tells me repeatedly, is for younger men nowadays, graduates 'who aren't even old enough to shave,' snapping at his heels leading to insecurity, fuelled by his employer, Gerard, who forever reminds Alan how highly trained and keen the younger generation are. He tells me that the only thing that keeps him sane is working with his best friend, our Best Man, Mike. We've talked about trying to pair Mike up with Ruth but Alan says Ruth would eat Mike alive and spit him out. He misjudges Ruth but he won't change his mind and anyway, Mike isn't Ruth's type. He has a low opinion of women borne through bitterness since his wife, Patsy, ran off with her personal trainer taking their son with them.

"Work was shit as usual," he grumbles. "Gerard wants me to go on a bloody course. I told him not to waste his money, no bloody course is going to make me better at my job, but he said if I don't keep up with the new software then he'll find a younger bloke who will."

"I've got my course coming up this

weekend, don't forget," I remind him. "Well, not actually a course but a team building thing for business women. The thought of it fills me with horror too, but we have to do these things, Alan. We have to keep abreast of change or fall behind and be trampled on."

"Yeh. Whatever." He drains his glass and burps.

"Charming."

"Better out than in, heard about a bloke that died once from trapped wind," he burps again and turns up the volume on the television, and so ends our conversation.

2

It's finally Thursday. The time is twelve fifty and I'm inside the Value Inn, waiting for a lift car to take me to the third floor, room 311 where my delectable fire fighter Simon awaits.

I don't think I have ever felt so sexually charged, my new lace panties are damp with my arousal and my heart is pounding. I'm wearing a long navy woollen coat, which reaches to the tops of my black knee length boots. Beneath the respectable woollen façade a scandalously short gold vest dress clings to my curves and allows my breasts to spill forth almost to the nipples. Lace topped stockings are suspended from my newly purchased black suspender belt and garters. I feel like a whore. I *am* a whore. My entire ensemble was hastily purchased yesterday and kept secreted away in carrier bags in the boot of my car. Changing at work had been a challenge but I succeeded in racing from the office to my car without being seen, and here I am now – squirming and tugging down the hem of my dress from beneath the flaps of my coat, my work clothes folded neatly on top on my sensible shoes in a small navy holdall at my feet.

I knock gently on the hotel door as a flake of paint falls away. Three knocks. Wait. Another knock. Our code. The stranger releases the lock and the door opens. There stands a treat to behold, naked except for a white towel, which hangs loosely from his hips and is tied to the side. He's a classic 'Y' shape - broad set shoulders tapering down to narrow hips with sharply defined pectoral muscles and solid biceps, I lick my lips keenly, thinking that all my Christmases have come at once.

"Simon. Hi." I can't think what to say to him, suddenly embarrassed, my face flushing fiercely. I place the holdall and my handbag on the wooden luggage rack next to the door.

He doesn't reply, instead he's all hot breath and sultriness, as he pushes the door closed, stands behind me and places his fingertips lightly on either side of my neck.

I shiver in momentary alarm, reminding myself how little I know of this man. His fingers slip beneath the lapel of my coat and he pulls it from my back. I outstretch my arms to aid the coat's removal and he drops it to the cheap green patterned carpet, where it pools at my feet. He's still behind me and I feel the prickle of tiny electric shocks coursing down the trail of my spine.

"Sit on the bed." He commands and I step forward to the queen size bed and sit on the edge, revelling in his assertiveness and keen to comply.

"Wow," I say nervously. "Aren't you the bossy one."

"Sshh." He puts his finger to his lips. *Oh my*.

The ache between my legs is becoming unbearable and my breathing quickens in anticipation of what this man will do to me. He saunters with a slow, sexy swagger to where I sit and my eyes travel from the trail of dark hair at his perfectly formed upper pubic area to his navel, up to his beautifully sculpted chest, which is matted with course black hair. This man is a God. I've won the sex lottery, and I intend to spend my winnings during the next two hours before I'll have to leave to collect my children. Guilt surges through me like a tsunami as I think of the family I am betraying, but Simon forces my legs apart with his knee and guilt gives way to lust once more.

Gazing longingly at Simon's ruggedly handsome face, I note that he appears younger than his profile age of thirty-eight, by a good ten years. His youthful looks belie his manly expertise as he sinks to his knees between my quivering legs. He leans forward and his mouth finds mine. His tongue pushes between my parted lips and probes inside my hungry mouth. He bruises my lips with his brutal kiss and I reach forward and entangle my fingers in his bushy black hair, tugging roughly at the roots until he moans. His hands clutch at my breasts, releasing them from their Lycra restraint. His mouth leaves mine - I'm panting and wanting, my hands pushing his head downwards demandingly. "Wait," he rasps, as his expert mouth finds my throbbing nipple and sucks and flicks it so tantalizingly slowly.

"I want you *so* badly," I groan. My fingers travel down from the nape of his neck to his back where they glide over the beading sweat that is forming.

"You're so hot Rosie." He pulls away from my nipple, leaving it bereft, and trails his hot tongue down to my navel, his towel falling away exposing his lean buttocks and colossal manhood. *Oh thank you Lord ... he's huge!*

Self conscious, suddenly, I try to suck in my jelly belly, extending my arms behind me I rest back onto my hands so that my midriff is elongated, and the small folds of tummy fat become less obvious. He roughly pulls off my panties before his tongue continues its journey southward. My eyes close in utter rapture, as his fingers part my cleft and hold me open and exposed. His mouth encompasses my clitoris and sucks before his teeth catch the tip of me making cry out in ecstasy. Collapsing back onto the bed, my fists grasp the white cotton sheets as he circles and flicks at my sweet spot with his tongue.

"Your cunt is dripping for me," he murmurs appreciatively as he slides two fingers into my wetness.

"Oh. Please. Don't Stop." I pant at the blissful sensations from the unfamiliar attention my body is receiving. A third finger slides in, lubricated by my juices and all three of his probing digits massage the sweet bundle of nerve endings deep inside me while his thumb rubs me so exquisitely. I feel myself building, and he senses my imminent orgasm and quickens his rubbing and massaging, thrusting now with his hand, his mouth on my thigh, biting into my flesh and I'm lost in the crescendo of pleasure which ripples and spasms, drenching his fingers in my liquor. As I feel the tremors subsiding I lay panting on the bed feeling a release which is alien to me in its' completeness. "Holy fuck," I gasp, breathlessly.

"Suck me." The cold instruction cuts through my stupor and I raise my trembling body from the bed. He's standing before me now, between my legs still. His magnificent cock stands erect and hard, the veins along its length throbbing as he thrusts his hips toward my eager mouth. Sliding off the bed to my knees, I grip the backs of his thighs pulling his waiting organ to my mouth. He grabs my hair with both hands and forces my head toward his groin. The shiny head of his enormous cock is almost too large for me to take him into my mouth. I flick my tongue across his crown and eagerly lap up the salty bead of fluid, which has formed on the cleft of his tip.

"Yes. Take it all, you fucking slut." His hands force my head nearer still so that his pulsing cock enters my mouth causing me to gag as it hits the back of my throat. He is so immense but I work him with my mouth, sliding him past my lips, sucking hard and working his root with my cupped hand. His enraptured moans reassure me that I'm pleasuring him well. My head bobs as I work his cock but my breath catches as Simon pulls sharply on the hair at the nape of my neck, tugging me away from his groin. He slips from my mouth but continues to pull my hair so that I'm forced to stand, aroused by the hair pulling, the pain blending seamlessly with the pleasure.

I lean into him and kiss him, seeking assurance that he's pleased with me. Pulling away from my kiss, he grasps my shoulders and spins me around so that I have my back to him once more. Still using the tug of my hair to guide me, he forces me forward over the edge of the bed so that my ass is in the air. Releasing my hair, he moves close to me so that I can feel the tickle of his pubic hair against my buttocks and the hard rod of his penis pressing into my ass. I feel him reach to the nightstand, hear the tearing of foil and he slides a condom onto his hardness. Panic sets in at the vulnerability of my most private cavity but instead, the head of his cock presses into my pulsing vagina, stretching my walls until, with one sharp thrust, I feel him fill me so full that I fear he'll tear me apart.

His thrusts are purposeful and fierce and, in just a few short moments, he cries out my fake name, "Rosie. Oh shit. Here it comes," and he pumps and releases his load as his sweating torso arches back in frenzy. "Fuck, you're good" he praises as he pulls out, removes his condom and tosses it into the waste paper bin.

I crawl up onto the bed and pull the sheet over my glistening body, feeling suddenly self-aware, exposed but deliciously used. Actually I feel dirty, as though I've been a mere vessel for his climax. *Is this a good feeling or a bad feeling? It feels both.* This inner conflict is not what I envisaged, and yet it's entirely what I bought into when I began my illicit journey. Hearts and flowers and loving sentiments do not marry with uniform dating and extra marital affairs. Simon takes my hand and pulls me up from bed into his waiting embrace; my arms folding around his waist, cheek pressed to his moist chest. We're both flushed and the hotel room smells of sex.

"Shower with me, I've got to go in a minute," he orders curtly.

"So soon? I have another hour," I say, my eyes searching his for signs of a connection that surpassed just sex, yet finding none. Evidently a man of few words, I wonder whether he has much depth but then I remind myself that the purpose of our meeting wasn't for conversation.

The water is cleansing and goes part way to purging the dirtiness I feel within. "Will I see you again?" I ask tentatively, towelling my body dry. He's made no mention of repeating today's sleazy afternoon, which doesn't boost a girl's confidence.

"Yes, sounds good. I'll call you, I've got your mobile number," he promises.

"Only call between 9am and 3pm please," I'm suddenly concerned that Simon may call when I'm at home.

"No worries. Jealous husband?"

"You could say that," I frown. Alan would kill him. Or kill me, if he found out. *Or would he even care?* I wonder.

"Alright, I'll be careful. It'll have to fit round my shifts though," he replies.

I retrieve my work clothes and fresh underwear from the holdall and dress quickly, screwing the gold dress and slutty underwear into the holdall, boots on top.

"Very prim," says Simon, watching me while leaning against the wall by the door, towel still draped around his hips. "But I know what a whore you really are, don't I?"

"Isn't that a good mix?" I ask with a smirk curving my lips. "Prim on the outside, whore on the inside?"

"Oh yes. A very good mix," he purrs.

Buttoning my coat, I take a last look at my surroundings. The bland interior of the economy room does nothing to lessen the cheapness I feel in myself. We kiss briefly, Simon assuring me that he will be in touch in a few days, and I leave.

Sitting alone in my car in the school car park killing the hour until pick-up time I reflect on the afternoon, mentally flaying myself for being an adulterous slut. The enormity of what I have done overwhelms me and tears sting my eyes.

With the children on board, suppressing the forlorn sobs, which threaten to burst forth, I dutifully ask them about their day and resign myself to settling back in to my dull life. *What was I thinking? This isn't the answer, Beth,* I tell myself. If I do leave Alan, it needs to be because of his unreasonable behaviour, not because of my cheating. The children would never forgive me if I chose another man over their father and yet, having tasted the forbidden fruit, I'm not convinced I have the willpower to stop myself now.

Alan won't be home for another hour, which gives me time to hide the holdall at the back of my wardrobe, under a mound of shoes. I'll have to launder the clothes at the weekend, hide them amongst the school uniforms. Thankfully for me, Alan never gets involved in laundry duties.

Later, lying in bed in the darkness – with Alan snoring beside me – sleep evades me. My mind runs through today's encounter moment by racy moment. Feelings conflict from relief at not being caught, to arousal at the memory of the hair tugging, from fulfilment to deceit, from elation to despair. I ponder the idea of seeking counselling, it cannot be normal to feel so mixed up, but dispel the idea – there is no way I can add more pressure to my schedule, nor can I share these disreputable thoughts with another.

Eight thirty-five am. We are even later this Friday morning. Lack of sleep means I am running on zero energy. I shout at the kids to get in the car, forget Joe's book bag and forget to say goodbye to Alan. *Thank goodness it's nearly the weekend … except of course I have to drive all the way to Cornwall for the teambuilding thing.*

Arriving at work, I'm truly thankful for the peace and tranquillity my office affords me. Immersing myself in work takes my mind off the jumble of emotions, which plague my mind, and dip my mood. Our finances are under strain, the industry is doing well in spite of the recession, but we have to chase the work more than we used to and this requires additional advertising investment. We are fast outgrowing our offices and need more administrative staff. All of this pressure falls upon me, Ruth leading on the operational side of the business. I need to find the money, *but where?*

In need of a distraction, after three hours of number crunching, I click on the Google search engine. *What shall I search? Hair tugging? Caning? How quickly my mind degenerates!* I'm carried along on a web thread to the dark and lurid world of BDSM – bondage (and discipline), dominance (and submission) and sadomasochism (sadism and masochism) is but a small part of the comprehensive definition offered up by Wiki. It's a whole new world … and yet strangely familiar to me. *I'm a masochist.* There, I've said it, like an alcoholic at an AA meeting. *Hello, my name is Elizabeth Dove and I'm a masochist. It's been twenty-four hours since I last had my hair pulled and it's driving me crazy. I long for another drink of sadism, but I worry that another drink will lead to a real BDSM addiction. I've got kids, you see, and I'm a respectable woman. Nobody knows I long to be drunk on a good beating. Can you help me quit the habit?*

A BDSM dating site is displayed before me, tempting me shamelessly with free and instant membership. After hesitating and battling with my inner demons for fifteen minutes, it only takes five minutes to create my profile, after which I sit back and stare at the screen with trepidation and excitement. Just two minutes later, three men have viewed my profile - dominant men seeking submissive ladies. Opening a new frame, I search 'dominance and submission' online for clarification and confirmation that I can call myself 'submissive'. It seems that I do indeed fit that dynamic sexually, albeit in my fantasies if not in real life. *Beth Dove – submissive slut.* Actually, I'm no longer Beth Dove, technically I am now 'rosiesub', not imaginative but it hadn't already been claimed. The pseudonym enables me to separate my professional and personal life with my sordid desires and alter ego, this in turn lessens my inner conflict.

"Hey Beth. Are you busy?" I start at the intrusion, minimising the opened window on my desktop and turn to face Julie, the temp who is covering maternity leave.

"No. Not at all," I bluster. "What can I do for you?"

"Ruth asked me to make sure you've signed off the accounts before the weekend. Can I tell her you have?"

"Yes. Nearly done, thank you Julie."

Alone once more, I click on my profile and see I have unread mail. Intrigued by the name of the sender, SlaveMaster, I open the message and almost fall off my chair ...

Girl,

Master is interested in talking with this girl, despite the lack of information on her profile. Master is not interested in this girl for curiosity only however, I have decided I am going to turn you into the perfect slave. You will listen to everything I tell you and provide Master with all of the information I seek. This must be clearly understood by the girl.

I expect a reply to this message within 45 minutes of you reading it. You will include your description (which will be full and detailed). Your description will not be generic and will describe you as you look at this precise moment in time.

The girl will also tell Master of her current living arrangements, work and relationship status and a list of duties the girl will perform. You will reply in exactly 200 words.

SlaveMaster

When I can stop laughing enough to type, I daringly tap a humorous reply …

Dear SlaveMaster

Thank you so very kindly for your interesting and challenging email. I have my stopwatch ticking down the 45 minutes - so anxious am I not to fail you in this first task, which you have so generously set me.

I am tall with longish blonde hair and blue eyes. I am wearing nothing at all because I stripped all of my clothing off the minute I read your message to me, such was my excitement and eagerness to please you.

My living arrangements currently are that I reside under a bridge, which is exceptionally cold currently, not least right now, void of my clothes as I am. No sacrifice or hardship is too great though to please you Master. I am fortunate in so far as I have full internet connection under this particular bridge, thanks to the hot-wiring I did on the nearby streetlight. My years spent in the Women's Remand Prison served me well and I am glad that I studied hard on the electronics course when I wasn't being ravaged by the plethora of lesbian inmates.

My relationship status, Sir, is that I am single.... technically, I am still married but he is likely to remain in prison for another twenty years unless he makes parole but after the last time he got caught (that wasn't my fault, I genuinely thought I was helping in turning him in), they said they were throwing the book at him. In hindsight I guess I shouldn't have hidden him under the stairs for those two long years, he may have got off more lightly.

So, Sir, I digress. To summarise, I am keen to drink from a dog bowl and lick your shoes until they shine brighter than the sun itself. Just say the word and I and my 13 children will be right there...

Yours respectfully,

Rosiesub

Within five minutes, I receive a reply from the jerk…

Girl,

Thank you girl, unfortunately it wasn't 200 words, so I couldn't read it.

What a weirdo! I sign out of my profile and get back to finalising the accounts, in need of some welcome normality. I may be sick, but I'm not *that* twisted. I wonder when I will hear from Simon and, in fact, whether I want to hear from him. I have a husband, healthy children and a good business – what more could I need?

When we arrive home, after school, Joe hands me a letter from his form teacher, advising me that Joe has been unacceptably late on three occasions this week and two last week. He asks if there is a valid reason for this tardiness and offers to meet with me to discuss Joe's progress – or lack of it. I fold the letter and tuck it in my briefcase. I will deal with this on Monday.

By the time Alan returns home from work at six-thirty, my overnight bag is packed ready for the morning and dinner is ready to serve.

We sit, as a family, at the kitchen table, Alan and the children devouring the lasagne, while I pick at my food with my fork but eat very little, my stomach in knots.

"Not hungry?" Alan observes.

"No. I think I'm getting nervous about tomorrow. I don't like meeting lots of new people, or doing a long journey alone." I rest my fork on my plate, replete.

"So who else is going then?" He quizzes.

"A bunch of egotistical Alpha females I suspect. My idea of hell, but Ruth and I agreed that I'd go. You don't mind do you?"

He cocks an eyebrow, apparently surprised at the request for approval. "Do what you like," his reply dismissive and cold.

"Nice to know I'll be missed," I quip.

"No doubt there'll be some blokes there too," he adds, ignoring my comment.

"Alan," I sigh, "it's a Women In Business event … the clue's in the name … *women*."

"Yeh right, it just seems odd to me." He scrapes the remaining lasagne from his plate into the food recycling bin, and crashes his plate and cutlery into the sink then leaves the kitchen.

"Oh piss off," I hiss under my breath.

3

Saturday morning, and I have made an early start on the long drive to Cornwall. The 'Women In Business' team-building weekend event - *why on earth did I put my name down for that?* I reflect. *As if I don't have enough to do, I now have to surround myself with alpha females, up to my arse in mud in Cornwall, of all places, where I feel sure everyone drinks cider and is inter-bred.*

Not only that, Alan is clearly convinced I'm making up the whole event and am in fact planning a liaison with another man. I worried last night that he'd found out somehow about

Simon, but then assured myself that he'd have gone crazy if that had been the case. Satisfied that he has no idea what I did two days previously, I made a show of kissing him goodbye this morning and telling him I would miss him.

As I drive west on the A35, the rain sets in. My journey to Cornwall should take three hours and twenty minutes according to Google maps and I'm glad that I set off early.

I pick up the M5 and the motorway is quiet. I relish the peace and solitude of my journey. A night away from Alan will be refreshing. I call my mother on hands free and have a chat to her, I haven't seen her as much as I should lately and it's good to talk to her. My mother lives only two miles from our house and is a considerable help with the children, for which I'm eternally grateful. She's seventy-four and has lived alone since Dad succumbed to prostate cancer twelve years ago. I make a mental note to treat my mother to a spa day some time soon.

Mum seemed quiet on the phone, when I

cut the call and reflect on our conversation I think about Dad and by the time I pass Exeter, I'm feeling melancholy.

Turning on the radio, I flick through the channels and settle upon an upbeat tune in the hope of raising my spirits before stopping for a strong cup of coffee and a bathroom visit near Launceston.

The pub I find is a traditional thatched inn, which is several hundred years old and very quaint. As I enter it feels as though one hundred eyes are upon me, all viewing me as a trespasser. I pay for the coffee and a cheese and pickle sandwich and find a table near the door, feeling nervous. I wish now that I'd cancelled my booking for the event, not relishing spending twenty-four hours with a bunch of strange women.

Although aware that outwardly I appear to be a competent entrepreneur, I seriously lack confidence and frequently doubt myself. I wear so many hats: mother, boss, wife but the saying 'jack of all trades, master of none' is a mantle I feel fits me well. *Who is the real*

Elizabeth Dove? I used to love to paint, before the children came along. I used to write poetry. *What happened to that carefree girl? Where and who is the real Elizabeth Dove now?*

I finish my lunch and return to my car feeling refuelled and ready to face the day ahead.

Shortly before two o'clock, after traversing dangerously narrow country lanes, the satellite navigation system on my dashboard tells me I've arrived at my destination. Indicating a right turn I drive past a pair of stone pillars on which stand two stone stags – weathered and chipped yet graceful with majestic horns, they look down on me with austere regard. The half-mile drive, lined with dense rhododendron, is staggeringly beautiful. Through the trees I glimpse acres of woodland, which gives way to paddocks with horses and fallow deer grazing. Beyond lies a jagged cliff, falling away to the sea beyond. I'm now driving slowly along the dirt and gravel track toward the most magnificent manor house I have seen. It takes my breath away.

I park next to a sleek white Range Rover, and cut my engine. Stepping out of the car onto the pale yellow gravel, I turn and gaze up at the façade of the enormous house, recalling from the literature sent to me that the main house is seventeenth century.

Taking my overnight bag from the trunk of the car, I walk toward the impressive entrance, feeling more positive about the weekend ahead. It will be therapeutic to have time away from Alan and this is a pretty cool place to hang out in. Above me I notice a 1634 date stone and a family crest featuring a dragon and shield. The house has a gothic style with stone mullioned leaded windows and I approach a vast arched doorway where I rap heavily on the wrought iron lion head knocker.

The door opens and, expecting a dusty old butler, I'm surprised to see a pretty dark haired girl ushering me in. The hall has an ornate plaster ceiling and fireplace with carved wooden over-mantel, on which I can see the date 1650. The mottled grey flagstone flooring is softened with ornate rugs in ochre and crimson hues. The walls are adorned with swords, axes and shields criss-crossed and glinting like metal rainbows in the sunlight, which streams through arched coloured leaded light windows, either side of the front door, that look as though they belong in a church. Each pane is adorned with a glazed image of knights, stags, rabbits and lions. It's so beautiful that it captures my attention for several moments.

"Stunning, isn't it?" the girl says.

"Breath-taking," I sigh.

"Come on, I'll show you through to the library. Most of the ladies are here already." The girl takes my overnight bag from my hand, then leads me through to the library, with dark oak panelling, carved pillars and yards of dusty books, it has a comfortable feel but not the silence one would expect of a library. The room is buzzing with the conversation of twenty or thirty women chatting in small groups.

Collecting a porcelain cup filled with milky coffee, I begin to introduce myself to a group of four women all dressed, like me, in jeans and pale pink sweatshirts with "Women Mean Business" slogan emblazoned across the front. The four women are all from the same organization, a PR company in London. We make polite small talk and, as one overly bleached blonde tells us about her latest client, I glance across the room. That is when I first see *him* and the room stands still. My breath catches and I feel myself flush.

I suggest that all women have an ideal man locked away inside our psyche – mine is tall, dark and handsome with a commanding and assertive demeanour. The man whose gaze I meet exceeds my dreams. He's tall, maybe six feet three or four inches and is dressed in blue denim jeans and an open necked blue checked shirt tucked in, the sleeves rolled half way up his strong, muscular forearms. His hair is jet black, yet speckled with silver flecks to the temples, giving him an air of maturity. He has coal dark eyes, framed by black eyebrows sculpted into a serious frown, and the broadest shoulders. Those shoulders are the kind onto which a woman could cry, cuddle, knead, and which would be consummately powerful. I estimate his age to be mid forties, but it is hard to be sure. As I stand transfixed by his maturity and rakish charm, his head turns and his gaze meets mine across the room. Blushing as a shiver passes through me, I avert my eyes. How ridiculous I must look, a grown woman beet red and trembling like a new born lamb. I turn away. *Play hard to get Beth! What are you thinking? Why would he be vaguely interested in me? I'm a married woman for heaven's sake!* I turn back to Bleached Blonde and laugh raucously at a droll story she is telling, then a hand touches my elbow and a spark courses through me. I turn and my cornflower blue iris lock on to his smoky dark hazel eyes with which he studies my plastic name badge pinned above my left breast.

"Elizabeth Dove. Managing Director, Evershaw Dove Recruitment Agency. Very impressive title *Elizabeth*." His deep, sensual gravelly voice renders me speechless. He uses my full name, which no one has done for many years, and they way his lips form the letters, parting to reveal perfect white teeth and the hint of a tongue, makes me tingle. I am lost to him in that very moment. "And you are?" I enquire, trying to sound disinterested and aloof.

"Sebastian De Montfort. Delighted to meet you. Welcome to my humble home". So he is the owner of this incredible house. This man is a mythological deity. He could not be more perfect.

"Pleased to meet you too, it's a beautiful home."

"Thank you, Elizabeth. I look forward to personally showing you around. I'll see you later, do enjoy the afternoon," he's charming, beguiling … and oh so dangerous.

I'm blushing a deeper shade of crimson as his eyes, deep and serious, fix their gaze upon me and refuse to blink or look elsewhere. He looks so intense, so measured and controlled. His hand lingers on my arm just a moment too long, he holds my gaze a moment too long. Then, he's gone. I can still feel his touch as he turns to greet a tall brunette in uniform pink sweatshirt.

"Isn't he delicious," gushes Bleached Blonde.

"Delicious. Yes," I whisper.

We are ushered through a glazed door leading from the library onto a paved terrace overlooking a walled garden where we are divided into two teams. I know that we'll be mud running but I really don't understand what this means. I imagine we'll be jogging, or in my case most likely walking, getting very grubby and having a good gossip and giggle. It comes as rather a shock, therefore, when we are assigned a team coach who is a fearful dragon on whom I feel sure the De Montfort family crest was cast.

The troll uses a megaphone to launch her verbal assault upon us. We're coaxed, bullied and cajoled into sprinting across the expansive lawns and down the tree-lined driveway.

We're ordered to veer off road when we reach a giant oak, and are soon running, tumbling through woodland in a battle to traverse the boggy terrain, endeavouring to beat the other team to the finishing post.

The ground beneath our running shoes becoming increasingly tricky and I feel my right foot slip. Before I can stop myself I am face down in slimy mud and I wonder if this can possibly be any more humiliating. Apparently, it can as Bleached Blonde laughs mockingly as she passes me. I am motivated to get to my feet. My knee stings and I see that the right leg of my jeans is torn exposing a raw graze. I wince but refuse to show any sign of defeat or to let my team down so instead push onwards, spitting out a mouthful of dank mud. How I survive ninety minutes of this torture is beyond me but I do, and when we break through the trees and back onto the driveway I am immensely relieved until I see the other team already at the finishing post, sipping cognac from paper cups. Damn them all.

I limp behind my teammates, my knee finally saying enough is enough. Laying claim to my cognac, the pitiful looks by the winning team don't go unnoticed and my mood worsens. It's not improved by the further humiliation of De Montfort handing out winners' medals to the other team and losers' medals to my team.

Standing in line, ripped trousers, bloody knee, caked in mud with leaves in my hair and a forced smile on my face, the Adonis places a ribbon over my head, adjusting the medal so that it rests on my sternum. He pauses and regards me, his amused eyes slowly drinking me in, his lips curled in a poorly concealed smirk. "I realize mud has untold benefits for the skin, Elizabeth, but I do wish you had left a little of it behind."

I could punch his conceited face but I hold back my twitching fist. Thankfully he moves on down the line and I release the breath I've been holding as fatigue takes hold.

We drift back into the house and locate our bedrooms. Mine is a sizeable room with high, decoratively corniced ceilings and it is furnished tastefully with antique pieces in dark oak. The double bed in the centre of the room is a two-poster with canopy and is dressed with a gold damask comforter and matching stack of cushions. At the foot of the bed stands a chaise upholstered in rich olive green fabric on which sits my overnight bag. I unzip it and remove a short cream silk nightgown, draping it over the bolster cushions. Retrieving fresh underwear and carefully unfolding a silver crepe evening gown from the crushed confines of the bag, I lay out my evening ensemble before running a bath.

The hot water feels so good despite the gash on my knee stinging fiercely and I sink down until the water level reaches my chin and reflect on the afternoon. I can't seem to get Sebastian De Montfort out of my head, with his smouldering eyes and moodiness. *'Sebastian'* is such a classy name, so much more impressive than 'Alan.' I decide I want to find out more about the mysterious man and this evening's dinner will be the ideal opportunity so I determine to make an extra effort with my appearance, after all I have all the other women to compete with for his attention.

The hot bath improves my mood and eases my aching joints. I'm excited about the drinks reception and dinner that awaits us, and am eager to discover more about the mysterious Sebastian. I moisturise my entire body, luxuriating in my sumptuous surroundings and the precious time to myself. My trusty, magic support pants 'tragic knickers' as I like to call them, are a struggle to pull up but necessary for a smooth silhouette under my slinky silver dress. Slipping the evening dress over my head, the whisper light fabric falls softly over my hips and ends just below my ankles and is cut low at my décolletage.

I pad to the bathroom at the same time as reaching behind my back to pull up my dress zipper, pulling out the plug in the bath and then trying again to tug up the zip. The loud gurgling of the draining bath water through noisy old pipework drowns out the sound of the light knock on my door.

I'm standing in the bathroom becoming flustered and hot as the zipper catches in the fabric of my dress, and I lean forward against the washbasin, arching my back in an attempt to free the snagged zip when a figure appears in the steamed up bathroom mirror. Gasping in shock I spin around and face Sebastian who is leaning against the bathroom doorframe, arms folded with a smile playing across his lips, his eyes crinkled in amusement.

"Don't worry about knocking will you." I scold sarcastically, embarrassed once again at the state in which he finds me – hot, red faced and my gaping dress twisted and puckered.

"Actually, I did knock, but you didn't hear me. I bought you this." He holds a sticking plaster between his thumb and forefinger and waves it in front of me. "For your knee. Would you like me to put it on for you?" he cocks an eyebrow and is clearly enjoying the spectacle.

"No, I don't want you to put it on for me, I'm a big girl." I retort ungratefully. "But thank you… it was thoughtful of you."

He steps toward me, reaches to my side and places the plaster on the marble countertop next to the basin. The closeness of him makes me tingle and I breathe in his manly scent as he lingers for just a moment, his fingers grazing my bare arm. He hesitates and then places his hand on my shoulder and the touch of skin on skin sends further tremors through my core. "Turn around," he says, as his hand pulls my shoulder toward him and guides me so that I face away from him.

"What are you doing?" I ask, my redness deepening and my breath catching.

"Your zip, Elizabeth. Unless you prefer to come downstairs as you are? Those large pants would cause quite a stir I'm sure."

Could this be any more humiliating?

His finger touches the small of my back as he tugs at the waistband of my tragic knickers, pinging the fabric against my skin and the mortification is unbearable. *Yes it can be more humiliating, damn him.* "Just do the zipper up." I bark at him. "Thank you."

My curtness serves only to increase his enjoyment and the irritating man sniggers as he releases the fabric and pulls the fastener half way up ... oh so slowly. He takes my long hair in his hand and drapes it over my shoulder before gliding the zip home and his fingers brush the back of my neck as he gently tugs my hair back into place. Such tiny touches and yet the electricity that passes between us is incredible and I feel sure he senses it too. As I turn back to face him he lowers his eyes quite shamelessly to the ample cleavage on display and only averts his gaze when I tug the fabric up as I tut my disapproval. "Is there anything else?" I ask rudely.

He crosses his arms again and places a finger on his lips as he stares pensively into my eyes. "I think you'll do. Be downstairs in ten minutes," he replies and with that, he turns and leaves the room, closing my bedroom door firmly behind him.

I let out a deep sigh. *That went well,* I scold myself.

It is a delicious meal of venison followed by a warm pear tart with cream. The wines are divine and I feel my mood lifting with each glass. Dinner is served by the pretty young girl who I saw earlier. In addition there are three other, equally pretty young ladies waiting the table. All are wearing fitted black dresses, which sit above the knee – demure but sexy, their hair tied back into a neat chignon. Curious. I make a mental note to ask the handsome but arrogant Mr De Montfort about his choice in staff. Clearly he hasn't recruited solely on the basis of curriculum vitae!

I sit through a series of speeches and clap politely when an award is given to the woman seated to my left, who has been judged to be the highest achieving woman in business. By eleven thirty, the evening draws to a close. Tired ladies make their way to bed, and I sit alone in the now empty dining hall. The lights are dimmed and the remnants of candles flicker on the long elegantly dressed table.

I sip my fifth or sixth glass of red wine feeling deliciously mellow and survey my surroundings. The high ceilinged room is papered in rich ruby damask, and gilt framed oil paintings adorn the walls, suspended from ornate picture rails. Many are of hunting scenes while others are, I presume, De Montfort's long dead relatives. They look down at me with reproachful stares.

The dying embers of a fire still offer a warming glow from the oversized fireplace. I take my glass of wine and sit in front of the fire, my legs curled under me on a deeply piled rug. I close my eyes and imagine I am sitting in my own castle, while my prince waits for me in our bedchamber. I imagine what he will do to me when I retire to bed and a sense of longing encompasses me.

I jump as I hear movement behind me. I turn and look up and see Sebastian De

Montfort standing over me. He has a half smile and his eyes are studying me curiously. I am suddenly consumed by a feeling of guilt, at how attracted to him I am, and embarrassment that I am so relaxed in his home.

"Elizabeth, don't let me disturb you, I've been watching you," he says. Before I can stand, he places a hand firmly on my shoulder and tells me to stay seated on the floor.

He pours himself a glass of red wine and sits down beside me - his legs crossed and his right knee touching my leg. I shiver at the touch of his limb through the silky fabric of my silver evening gown. "Let me see your wounded knee," he demands firmly. My mouth drops open and I look aghast at him. He wants to look at my bare leg! My scuffed sore knee.

I shake my head and tell him that it's nothing, I have the sticking plaster on it, and it really isn't painful. I look at him and he is looking deeply into my eyes, a frown etched across his brow.

He doesn't speak for the longest time and then, when he does he says only "show me."

It is not a request, I realize, he is insistent. I hesitate but he leans forward, gently grasps the hem of my dress and slides the fabric up my legs, above my knees. I'm blushing deeply now but to my amazement, he kisses his fingers and softly lays his fingers onto the covered wound. I feel a thousand sparks coursing through my body and have an overwhelming and totally irrational desire to feel his fingers on my skin.

"You're flinching. Is it sore?" He asks.

"A little," I reply although it was the spark from his touch rather than pain, which made me flinch.

"Are you enjoying yourself?" The conversation is awkward.

"Having a lovely time, yes thank you," I reply.

"You did make me laugh, Elizabeth. You were a picture, covered in mud with leaves in your hair." He has that ridiculous smirk on his face.

"I'm glad I entertain you," I huff. "Be sure to book me next time you need a good laugh."

He leans forward and tucks a loose strand of hair behind my ear. "Your hair is so much prettier without the foliage," he is still mocking me and I cast him a frosty glare in return, trying not to let him see the profound effect his touch has on me.

"Perhaps if we hadn't been subjected to the wrath of the old bat that led our team, I wouldn't have fallen," I suggest, much to his amusement.

"Old bat?" His eyes are glinting roguishly.

"Yes, old bat," I say defiantly.

He throws his head back and laughs, a deep rasping laugh and I love the way his eyes crinkle.

"You're laughing at me *again*!" I protest.

"Not laughing *at* you, no. It's a long time since I laughed. You light up the room."

"What a lovely thing to say." I put my hand on his tentatively and I swear a spark crackled as our skin touched.

He stares at me until I look away. "Come with me, I promised to show you a little more of the house but it's late. The grand tour will have to wait until another time, but I will show you the heart of the house. Come." He takes my hand, pulls me to my feet and leads me from the dining hall. For a moment I wish he would take me upstairs and have his wicked way with me, but in fact he leads me past the vaulted oak staircase and through a door into a vast kitchen where flagstones pave the floor and a double range stove forms a somewhat wholesome focal point. I immediately love this room, it feels so homely and welcoming and I imagine laughter and conversation around the refectory style oak table, which sits in the middle of the room. It is indeed the warm heart of the house.

He directs me to sit on one of the two

heavy church pew benches, which are placed either side of the table and he lights a candle, which gives a soft ambient light.

I notice there are no staff around and presume they have finished their duties for the night. He offers me coffee, and puts a heavy copper kettle onto the range to boil. Leaning against the wall next to the range, his dark hazel eyes fix on mine. It's so hard to read what is going on behind those darkly lashed windows to his soul.

Feeling emboldened by the alcohol, I decide to interrogate my mysterious host. "Tell me about your staff, Mr. De Montfort, it's clear that you haven't hired them for their brains" *did I really say that?*

"Elizabeth," his repeated use of my full name reminds me of my childhood. "That's a strange question. I like to surround myself with beautiful things. Does that make you uncomfortable?" His answer takes me by surprise but affirms my belief that he beds these women.

"Not uncomfortable. No. However, it seems strange to only hire attractive young girls… unless you expect additional benefits than just waitressing." It must be the alcohol really fuelling my confidence, but I can't stop myself.

He regards me more coolly, and I see hardness in his eyes that I haven't noticed before. "And would it shock you if I did?" he asks.

What does that mean? Is that 'yes I do fuck them,' or 'no I don't'? I want to ask. I rarely know when to keep quiet and I never think before I speak and I simply can't let this go - I want to know more. I match his stare and reply curtly. "Naturally, it wouldn't bother me - I don't know you. I'm simply curious as to how you treat these poor staff of yours Mr. De Montfort". *That told him. Gosh how much have I drunk?*

His retort cuts me to the quick. "Firstly, Elizabeth, I am not *Mister* De Montfort. I am *Lord* Sebastian De Montfort, 9th Earl of Trevissay. You may call me Sebastian – even though, as you rightly say, you don't know me". *Oh please.* A LORD!

"Secondly, Elizabeth, those 'poor staff of mine' elect to work for me. It may be that the financial incentives are considerable, or it may be that I am a fabulous lover, either way it's really not your concern is it?" *Geez* that told me!

"Thirdly Elizabeth," *there's a thirdly?* "Do you take cream and sugar in your coffee?" A wry smile touches his lips and I notice how his eyes smile too. He could melt me with those eyes.

"I'm sorry, I've no right to pry. I think I've had way too much to drink." I apologise profusely and the atmosphere lifts a little.

"I forgive you. Actually, it's not as bad as you seem to think. Three of the young women were hired for the event this weekend. Only one lives in permanently." That makes me feel a little better. *Why do I care?*

"I see." I fiddle with a thin silver bracelet.

"That's pretty," he is by my side now. Admiring my wristlet, he lightly runs his index finger along its circumference, his thumb brushing across my skin as I hold my breath. Abruptly, he resumes his position by the range, taking the simmering kettle from the hob.

"It was a gift from my children last Christmas," I tell him, missing Joe and Bella badly.

Sebastian hands me a steaming cup of coffee and sits on the bench opposite me, leaning forward and resting his chin on his hands. "How old are they?"

"Joe's seven and Bella is seventeen." I sip the coffee gingerly.

"That's quite an age gap," he observes.

"Yes it is," I reply. "We had difficulty conceiving. Primarily because sex didn't happen very often."

"I see. I'd like to know more about *you*," he prompts. "Tell me why I see sadness when

I look into those beautiful blue eyes."

He takes me by surprise yet again. He seems so intuitive and yet I feel angry at his bluntness when he'd been so protective of his own privacy. I consider my reply. "Not much to tell. Married, two children, my own business, busy life." I sum up my life in one brief sentence.

Upon a frown, his lips form a stern thin line. "Thank you for the brief synopsis Elizabeth, now please tell me about *you*."

"Everything?" I ask incredulously.

"Everything." He confirms, resting back against the pew, his arms crossed.

I find myself telling this man, this stranger, my life story. There is something compelling about Sebastian and I feel safe, in danger, lustful, all of those feelings but mostly I feel compelled to do as he says. He listens intently without interrupting and with an expression on his face that is unreadable. After I have finished, and my coffee is cold, he sits back and sighs deeply. I wonder if I should have told him about my marriage, my loneliness and my feelings of rejection. He is not saying anything. *Say something.*

"Why do you stay with him? You deserve to be cherished Elizabeth." He reaches across the table and tucks a loose strand of hair behind my ear again, and it is such a gentle yet sensual gesture that I blush once more.

"It's not that easy to leave him. I don't think I'm the perfect wife either." Yawning, I begin to succumb to fatigue and the alcohol.

"Because something is a challenge, does not mean that one shouldn't rise to it, Elizabeth."

"You have no idea …" I begin to say but he interrupts me.

"You'd be surprised. However, it's late," he says. "You are tired. Go to bed now. When you leave tomorrow morning, I want you to give me your business card and we'll meet again soon."

"Aren't you going to tell me anything

about you? I'm not that tired."

He shakes his head. "Not yet. Get some sleep."

He is utterly infuriating yet completely addictive. "Ok," I agree meekly. "Goodnight Sebastian. Thank you for a lovely night."

Sebastian proffers his hand, which I take in mine. "It's I who should thank you," he whispers. "You are an intriguing woman, Elizabeth Dove. I'm very glad you're here."

"Me too." Still holding his hand, I stretch up and kiss him gently on the cheek. He touches his cheek with his fingertips and closes his eyes. When he opens them I see pain in his eyes – a bleakness that makes my heart ache for him, and I long to hold him tightly and kiss him properly.

"Good night." He steps away, my fingers slip from his and the moment is gone.

Feeling exposed to him, and regretful, I go to bed. My emotions are jumbled and I scold myself for letting my guard slip.

Tomorrow is another day – a line from my favourite movie 'Gone With The Wind' - and it's my mantra now. I'll think about these feelings tomorrow.

Climbing wearily into bed, it crosses my mind that I'm doing as I am told for once in my life. I'm going to bed and getting some sleep because I'm tired and because Sebastian told me to. Sebastian has a manner about him, which makes me want to obey him and to make him happy. I realise how refreshing it is for a man to make simple decisions for me. It is truly what I long for, what I need. Sleep comes easily.

My eyes open to a soft golden shard of sunlight on my pillow. Rubbing sleep away with balled fists, I reach for my phone and see that it's nearly seven o'clock. Able to focus now I gaze at my room, at the dusty splendour of days gone by. Puddled curtains made of a heavy ochre brocade pool on the floor – I don't recall closing the curtains last night yet they are closed this morning, except for a small parting at the top from where the morning sun steals in to dispel the gloom. I try to recall how much I drank last night, as I massage my temples, my head muzzy. With a languid stretch and deep yawn I think to myself that I could get used to waking in a room like this each morning. *Heaven.*

Washed, dressed in a skirt, cashmere sweater and knee high winter boots and, satisfied that I have packed all my belongings into my overnight bag, I leave my bedroom and set off in search of breakfast.

The gaggle of female chatter, tells me that my event colleagues are gathering in the dining hall. Looking forward to the peaceful drive home, I take a seat next to last night's top business woman. She is a gregarious character who is large both in personality and stature. Congratulating her on her business achievement, we chat while breakfast is served. She tells me that she received her award following the growth of her online business and I wonder how much she's worth although I don't like to ask, which is surprisingly polite and restrained for me.

"Love, have you met his Lordship yet?" she asks me. "He's a strange one. Doesn't usually rent out his house for anything so we are very honoured."

I can sense that there is gossip about to spurt forth, and I draw closer to her conspiratorially, hungry for information regarding Sebastian.

"When the 'Women In Business' organisers were viewing venues, this one had just been made available for the first time. If you ask me he must need the cash ... or the company of a houseful of women. Rumour has it that his wife's dead but he's one for the ladies. They always are, these rich country folk."

I recall the spurious attributes of his Lordship's staff team who served us last night. "I met him last night," I say and watch her raise an envious eyebrow. "He seems rather aloof and, frankly, I found him to be arrogant."

This appears to whet the woman's

appetite for gossip and she nods her head in agreement. "Arrogant or not, I bet half the women in this room wouldn't kick him out of bed if given half a chance. He's gorgeous."

This time I am in agreement with her. She shovels a gargantuan forkful of scrambled egg into her mouth. My mobile phone beeps, indicating that a text message has been received. Pulling it from my handbag I see that it is Ruth asking how the event has gone. No doubt she'll require a thorough debrief on the whole event, as she'd been disappointed she couldn't attend due to a clash of meetings. I note that I have received no text message or missed call from Alan or from fire fighter Simon, not that I had expected to hear from either, but I find still find it hurtful. It would be nice to be missed and thought of.

The bevy of irritatingly attractive waiting staff are placing hot plates of full English breakfast in front of us all, and I heartily tuck into the delicious sausages, bacon and eggs and enjoy two cups of English breakfast tea served in delicate porcelain cups.

Breakfast finished, our group begins to disperse and begin homeward journeys. I wonder if I'll see Sebastian again this morning, finding myself longing to see him one more time yet I can't fathom what it is about that bossy, arrogant, tall, dark, gorgeous man that has me so mesmerized.

I stand in the vaulted hallway and look around, hoping for the opportunity to thank our host and to see him once more but he does not appear. Seeing the member of his staff who greeted me yesterday, I take the opportunity to ask if he will be saying farewell to us.

"His Lordship has already left to take his morning ride," she tells me. *His Lordship.* It has an old fashioned ring to it.

The disappointment of not seeing Sebastian again weighs heavily on my mind, but I decide to leave my contact information for him, in the hope that he will get in touch. "Sebastian asked me to leave my business card for him." I hand my card to the girl and she places it on the mantel above the fireplace in the expansive entrance hall. "Please ensure he gets that card, and please tell him that Beth Dove says thank you and goodbye."

With a curt nod she walks away, her trim figure disappearing through the kitchen door and it strikes me how like a slave she is – timid, pretty, dressed in black and evidently completely controlled by her boss. I wonder if she is the one who lives in, a twinge of jealousy taking me by surprise.

As I pull away in my car I glance in my rear view mirror at the magnificent house and wonder if I will ever see it again... see *him* again.

4

On the long drive back my thoughts are filled with Sebastian. I run through what I recall of our conversation in the kitchen, wishing I hadn't opened up to him as I did. My loose tongue will get me in trouble one day, if it hasn't already. I feel so stupid.

I stop for lunch at Exeter and browse in the large shopping mall. In a lingerie shop, I buy myself the smallest, sexiest set of underwear that I have ever possessed. Not for Alan's enjoyment or for Simon's. I have bought them for me – I am going to be a sexier, more liberated me. *You're changing, Beth*

- about time too, I tell myself.

Joe runs to greet me as I close the front door. Putting down my bags, I scoop him in a tight embrace.

"I've missed you, little guy," I tell him.

"Have you brought me a present?" He asks hopefully.

"No Joe. Mummy hasn't been on holiday, I've been working."

"Dad says you've been off 'on a jolly'," Joe huffs.

"Does he now. Well Dad's wrong."

Alan is sat at the computer, under the stairs in the tiny recessed study area, which has space only for a small desk and chair. His eyes remain fixed on the screen as I breeze past him to the kitchen. "You're back then," he observes brusquely.

"It would seem so. Yes," I reply cattily.

"Good time?"

"Not really. Pretty much as expected – loud women, lots of mud, draughty old house. How are the kids?"

"Fine."

So ends another conversation. I take my bags upstairs, unpack and take the laundry, including Thursday's gold dress and underwear, to the washing machine.

Deciding on an early night, it seems a good opportunity to talk to Alan about my feelings. We can't continue as we are, both bitterly unhappy. "Alan, I've been thinking about us."

"I'm tired, Beth." He turns his back to me and pulls the duvet up protectively.

"I'm tired too. Look, please will you reconsider couples counselling? Lets at least try and fix our marriage if we can … before it's too late?"

"We've had this discussion countless times," he mumbles. "I'm not going air my dirty laundry with a stranger."

"So, you don't want to save our marriage?"

"To be perfectly honest, Beth, no. It's too late."

I feel I've tried. There is little more I can do to help us. With a heavy heart, I lie in the darkness until the first light of dawn when I drop into a fitful sleep.

It's Monday morning, at the office. Ruth is on the telephone barking at some unfortunate soul. I make myself a steaming cup of coffee and sink down onto the couch in my office, feeling weary and reflective.

"Tell me, how did it go this weekend?" Ruth is standing in doorway. I beckon for her to sit beside me and recount the events of last forty-eight hours. She is horrified at the sound of the mud running and the relief that she wasn't able to take part is clear on Ruth's face.

"Oh, and I met a man." I drop the bomb

and wait for the aftershock.

Ruth raises her eyebrows with a look of mock horror on her face.

"Why am I not surprised?" She sighs, rolling her eyes.

"He was the most frustrating man I have ever met," I continue. "He had this infuriating way of extracting all my deepest, darkest secrets and yet wouldn't tell me anything about himself."

"Ooh, sounds very intriguing," says Ruth. "Is he attractive?"

"Ruth, he is seriously *gorgeous!* Tall, dark hair – greying at the temples – and he has the darkest eyes. And get this ... he's a *Lord!*"

This instantly grabs her attention, and she lets out a loud 'whoop!'

I quickly put out her flames by adding that, of course, I won't ever see him again and in any case he is allegedly a womaniser.

"Aren't they all," she adds and I have to

agree with her. She takes a long hard look at me, detecting the changes I feel.

"I can't recall seeing you like this before Beth." Ruth knows me too well. "If I didn't know better, I'd say that you really do *like* this man. You seem… different."

Ruth is right. I *feel* different. I haven't felt this way for a very long time. For the first time in 17 years, a man is interested in *me*. Not Beth the boss, Beth the wife, Beth the mum, or even Beth the whore, but *me*. I want to see Sebastian again.

"Be careful, Beth," she warns. "If you start something with this man, and Alan finds out …"

"Ruth. It's nothing, I'm not having an affair but it's nice to be noticed. It's good to feel like a woman instead of a drudge."

"I know, love. I know things are bad at home, but just be careful. You've a lot to lose."

The rest of my week is busy. My days are

filled with meetings and running errands for the kids. I barely have a moment to myself.

I've heard nothing from Simon since we met last week, and that only serves to confirm that I made a huge mistake in doing what I did and today I deleted my profiles on the uniform dating website and the BDSM site. I feel neglected and miserable.

It's Thursday afternoon, and I am putting on my coat to leave my office when my mobile phone bleeps with a received text message. I pick it up from my desk and hurriedly check the message, certain that it will be from Bella as I am late collecting her from her dance lesson, secretly hoping it may be from Simon.

Elizabeth I enjoyed our chat. Meet me for lunch. Sebastian.

I gasp. It's from *him*! A sudden tingle traces from my belly and travels downwards. Lunch! *Typical man,* I think – he's in Cornwall and I'm in Dorset and he wants me to meet him for lunch. Whilst I am relieved that Slave

Girl gave him my business card, I am now filled with nervous trepidation at the sight of his text message.

Reading the message again, I note that there are no pleasantries in the text such as 'x' at the end or indeed a cordial invitation to lunch. It's a *summons* to lunch. I feel resentment building inside me, I am used to being in charge and more than fed up with being taken advantage of.

Dear Sebastian, thank you for your kind invitation but as you live in Cornwall, which isn't exactly down the road from me I hardly think I can meet you for lunch?! Beth.

I press 'send'. *That told him*, I think smugly. Then, I am filled with self-doubt, *why was I so rude?* Too late, the phone whooshes as it sends my text. Almost immediately my phone beeps.

How do you know I'm not coming to Dorset on business?

Oh crap! I hadn't thought of that, in my

mind he lazed around his mansion, only leaving his slave girl to go riding each morning. I text him back.

So, are you in Dorset on business?

Again a swift reply.

No. Meet me outside your office 1.30pm tomorrow. Sebastian.

He has my business card. Of course he knows where my office is. The calendar on my phone contains my carefully ordered life, and I note that I have an eleven thirty meeting tomorrow, with a new client. *Double crap.* That should be ok though, I realize. If I wrap the meeting up promptly, it is only twenty minutes away.

What am I thinking? How can I possibly have lunch with that man. But lunch is just lunch, right? It's not as if I'm going to jump into bed with the man. Though the idea sends that same tingle down my body again. *It is just lunch.*

"Hurry up kids, I have a busy day!" I

bellow up the stairs to my children. It's eight fifteen already and I need to get going. My mind is full of thoughts of my lunch today with Sebastian.

I check my appearance in the mirror in our bedroom for the umpteenth time. I've tried on three different outfits and settled for the black pencil skirt, white fitted blouse, barely black stockings and black heels. Very business like but also a little sexy, I note as I see how the skirt and blouse show off my curves. *I'll do.*

Alan eyes me suspiciously as we exchange brief farewells in the kitchen. "You look dressed up again, going somewhere nice?" he enquires with a discernable hint of sarcasm.

"I have an important meeting with a potential new client," I tell him, quite honestly. " I want to make a good impression, it's a valuable contract."

He doesn't look convinced. "Amazing how many *meetings* you have recently," he sneers.

"Alan. I run my own business. Of course I attend business meetings. Stop the crap."

"Do whatever you fucking want," he snarls hatefully.

A pang of guilt pricks my conscience as I dash out of the front door, scooping up my briefcase and yelling at the children to get into the car, we're late again.

I reach my office at nine fifteen, having deposited the children at their schools and fought with the rush hour traffic. Ruth is waiting for me in my office with coffee ready for me. We discuss today's meeting and Beth tells me that she will be tied up in interviews today. I neglect to mention my lunch appointment, knowing that she would be shocked. Ruth leaves my office and I sit down at my desk and power up my computer. I check my emails and reply to any that are urgent. Then my thoughts wander to Sebastian. He seems so ... *dominant.* My curiosity wins out again, and I click on Google Search, typing in the word 'dominant' and the words 'man' and 'woman'. The first search heading "The Truth About Men Dominating Women" leads me to a website which discusses domestic abuse. I hit the 'return' key and select the next link:

Why every woman wants to be dominated by a man

Dominant men exude power, are comfortable in their own skin and with their own identity. They are never weak and never hesitate nor seek approval from others either in a social situation or in the work place. Women are attracted to those with power. While most men aim for women with looks, women need a man who is assertive, independent, strong minded and a leader.

Women have a deep-rooted instinct that draws them toward dominant males and this inner urge cannot be suppressed – it is a part of their very survival.

My friends and family would consider me to be the leader in my life, upon who so many are reliant, including men. Yet I can relate to the article, as I'm tired of leading and would dearly love to be led. To have some of the decision-making taken from me would be, frankly, heaven. A burden lifted. A cloud dispersed, and yet to hand over control to another would require complete trust, and I don't know if I am capable of trusting unquestioningly.

My meeting runs smoothly, but I find it difficult to concentrate. I have butterflies in my tummy and a growing sense of panic for so many reasons.

I have no idea where we will be going for lunch and, when I get back to my car, I take out my phone and run a search on local restaurants. I wonder if we shouldn't be going somewhere further afield – somewhere where there is no risk of being seen by one of Alan's friends or associates. That makes me feel more guilt than ever. *It's just lunch Beth*, I scold myself. I decide upon a bistro on the other side of town, which has excellent online reviews.

I have time to dash into my office and

reapply my lipstick and a dash of perfume, and use the cloakroom before my watch tells me it's one thirty.

I step out of our office building and rest against the wall. It's a cold afternoon - the autumn sunshine takes the chill from the air, but does little to settle the nervousness I feel. My eyes dart from one end of the street to the other and back, scanning the faces of those going about their business, in case Alan is watching me. It's irrational but then Alan has seemed irrational and increasingly antagonistic. Ruth's warning rings through my head. *Be careful Beth.*

Then I see Sebastian. He's walking toward me with a confident swagger, and he's even more gorgeous than I recall. He wears a camel, wool overcoat with the collar turned up and his shoulders look so very broad. He has dark sunglasses on to shield his eyes from the low autumn sun, and I can't tell if he is looking at me but I sense that he is. The familiar warmth oozes through my core and my pulse quickens at the sight of him.

"Elizabeth, so good to see you again," he says as he grips my arms, pulls me closer and kisses me on both cheeks. I am a quivering wreck now.

"It's good to see you too Sebastian," is my lame response, but I mean it. It is *so* very good to see him again. "I thought we could try a French bistro across town," I suggest. "The reviews are very good and…"

He puts a finger to my lips to silence me. "I've booked a table for us Elizabeth, at a very fine hotel I know. It's twenty minutes drive from here, and the food is excellent. When you get to know me a little better you will learn to trust my judgment, and you will know that I take the lead in all things. Let's walk to my car."

All things? What is that supposed to mean? I wonder. However, I like the sound of that - such a refreshing change. I am grinning and, feeling bold, I slip my arm through his as we walk to his car. I am a new woman already. I feel it. I don't notice the red Ford Focus parked in the side road, nor do I notice Alan sitting at the wheel watching us walk by.

We walk to Sebastian's car, the sleek white Range Rover that I had seen at the house. He holds the door open for me and I climb in, relishing the feel of the leather against my legs. Sebastian starts the engine and we join the flow of traffic heading onto the ring road.

The Ford Focus indicates, and nudges into the traffic three cars behind ours.

Sebastian presses an illuminated button on his dash and the car is filled with stirring music, which I recognize to be Pachelbel's Canon in D Major – a beautiful piece in which I lose myself as I gaze at the road ahead. Neither of us feels the need for words as we become absorbed in the music.

The Ford maintains its' position behind us – out of Sebastian's view but following us still.

Arriving at The Willows hotel, I am instantly impressed. It's quietly elegant but not pretentious, and I wonder if Sebastian has been here before as he leads us confidently and knowingly through the foyer and into a small, intimate bar adjacent to the restaurant.

Sebastian places a hand on the small of my back and I feel the sparks again and catch my breath. He guides me to a large tartan covered couch, and we sit. The couch is aged and the cushions soft, and we sink down together, his leg pressed against mine, his elbow touching my breast. He doesn't adjust his position to put more distance between us. A waiter soon approaches and Sebastian orders a bottle of Pol Roget.

The waiter pours a little of the champagne into sparkling crystal flutes. It's deliciously chilled, and as I sip the dry bubbles, I feel relaxed with this man. I feel I've misjudged him, there is no hint of arrogance today. He seems jovial and approachable, I decide to strike now and launch into interrogation part two. "Sebastian, the other night, in your kitchen, I told you things that I haven't told anyone before and yet I know so little about you. Tell me everything - about your life, work and your family. Please. You're so mysterious." I wonder how much he will divulge to me. By 'family' of course I'm hoping he won't spring a lover and children on me and, of course, I await confirmation that his poor unfortunate wife is dead.

He sinks further into the cushions, placing his left arm along the length of our seat, so that his hand rests behind my back, making me shiver with the nearness of him.

"There's such a lot to tell you, Elizabeth." His fingers fidget with the upholstery piping. "I'm very fortunate because I've inherited a title, land and the wonderful house but I've also inherited a burden of responsibility, and that burden is not an easy cross to bare."

This is intriguing. Nodding, I urge him to continue.

"But, inquisitive lady, you will just have to be patient. I'll tell you more about me, but not now." *What?* He is indeed the most infuriating man I have met.

"Sebastian," I whine, "I'm not a patient

person. At least answer a question for me please," I am not letting him off that lightly.

He raises one of his dark eyebrows at me, and his arm moves from behind me into a more defensive, arms crossed pose. I'm pushing my luck but I press on.

"I understand you've been married and…I think your wife passed away…oh gosh that sounds insensitive and I don't mean it to…" I'm digging a huge crater sized hole for myself but again I press on. "I just wondered if you are on your own or if you have a special person in your life?" *Shoot me now. Why don't I just come out and ask him if he's single and if he wants to come to bed with me*, that's how he will interpret my stupid question.

He's looking at me with a smirk on his face *damn him*. "Well now, you speak your mind don't you Elizabeth? I can see that you've been listening to gossip but, yes, you're right – my wife Libby did sadly die. To answer your second question, I've many special people in my life but I'm unattached romantically."

I have no idea what he means. He is staring at me as he sips from his glass.

"That's what you mean, isn't it?" His lip curls and he cocks an eyebrow. "Why didn't you just ask if I'm available?"

The champagne spits from my mouth as I choke on his audacity. "No." I counter. "That's *not* what I meant." Recovering my composure, I straighten a cushion and put my glass on the polished table in front of us.

"I'm sorry to hear about your wife, truly." Poor man. I wonder how she died. I decide to keep quiet and drink more champagne and thankfully we are ushered into the restaurant for lunch.

"Come. We'll talk more over lunch." He takes my hand and we leave the bar with our hands entwined and the touch of his skin on mine makes me ache with need.

Over lunch of sea bass, conversation flows freely. We chat about more light-hearted topics such as my work, and he tells me a little about his house and life in

Cornwall. He tells me about the tenant farmers who provide the income to maintain his estate. He looks worried when he tells me that, over the years, the tenants – some of whom have lived on his estate for generations – gradually leave, as farming is hit by the recession and EU subsidy reductions. He talks freely, but doesn't divulge a great deal of personal or intimate information about himself. He seems a very private man but also a deep thinker, and is incredibly intelligent. Lunch is divine and I can see why Sebastian chose this place. After coffee Sebastian requests the bill and I offer to share the bill, but he insists on settling the bill himself. "One thing you will accept is that I'll never allow a woman to pay. Get used to it because it won't change." *How refreshing.*

As we walk out to Sebastian's car I freeze in absolute horror. Alan is leaning against the bonnet of Sebastian's car and he looks furious. I feel light headed and nauseous. Alan marches towards us, his face masked in fury.

5

Eyes boring into my very soul – if he could kill me with a glare I would be breathing my last. "You cheating bitch," he spits venomously at me. "I thought you looked too fucking dolled up for a meeting you lying whore."

I want to run, but Sebastian places his hand firmly on my arm and I feel him straighten and tense beside me.

"Stay where you are. I'll handle this," he warns me.

"Who the fuck's this?" Alan shoves Sebastian's shoulder. Fearing Sebastian, or Alan, may hit out I stand between the two men. I'm shaking.

"Alan for God's sake. I've had lunch with a colleague that's all"

He's not listening to me. He's beating his fists against his legs menacingly. "Don't fucking lie to me, you slut."

Sebastian steps forward, pushing me aside so that he squares up to my husband. His face contorts with a rage that far exceeds Alan's and for a moment, Alan looks scared. Unsure what to do and consumed by panic, I turn and run back into the hotel wanting to escape.

Tears streaming down my hot cheeks, I seek solace in the ladies' cloakroom. I lock myself into a cubicle and sob. I'm so unhappy. I love my children and I don't want my life with them to change but, if I was happy, I wouldn't be having lunch with Sebastian. It's all so confusing and I feel wracked with guilt, but also angry with Alan for following and humiliating me. My unhappiness, compounded by stress, causes the tears to spill forth as I lean against the cubicle wall.

After a few minutes, I hear the door to the ladies cloakroom open and the sound of heavy footsteps cross the tiled floor and I see, through my tears, a pair of black shiny shoes beneath my cubicle door.

"Open the door, Elizabeth."

Opening the door I look up at Sebastian and see his face full of concern and compassion, and this makes me sob again.

He pulls me into his arms and tightly embraces me and it feels so safe, so comforting to be held by his strong arms, my tear stained face against his chest. He puts a finger under my chin and raises my face and tells me not to cry. Alan has gone, and he whispers to me that all will be ok. I want to believe him. He lowers his head and kisses each of my eyes, and then his lips find mine. I kiss him too then, passionately and deeply, my mouth hungry for his. Our tongues meet and we taste each other for the first time. I press against him harder, and his arms tighten around me. I feel his hardness then against me, and a current of excitement runs down my spine and all the way down to my sex.

Our lips part and I feel breathless as my chest heaves. My raw desire for this man shocks and shames me and yet I want more. I want all of him, to feel him inside me.

"Elizabeth I want you more than I've wanted anyone in my life. I know you want me too," he rasps. "I want to protect you. To take all this away from you."

"I don't know, Sebastian, but … I'm married. Oh God, what a mess." The tears come again.

"Darling, you don't know me yet, you're right, but you will. We'll get to know each other. Come." He takes my hand and leads me to the basins where he runs a paper towel under the cold tap and wipes away my tears and black streaks of mascara from beneath my eyes.

The door opens, and an elderly lady enters the cloakroom. She gasps when she sees a man in there and hastily retreats back through the door, flapping disapprovingly. I look at Sebastian and we laugh! Goodness knows what I have to laugh about but I can't help it, my laughter verges on hysteria.

As we leave the hotel and walk back to Sebastian's car, my eyes dart across the car park, searching for Alan's car but it's not there. Driving back to my office, I wondering what I'm going to do – *can I go home?* I haven't technically done anything wrong and certainly not what Alan believes. The kiss was wrong, yes, but it was not adultery, but will Alan believe anything I say? *What if he boots me out of the house … what will happen to the children? Oh fuck, what a mess.*

Intuitively, Sebastian reaches across and lays a hand on my knee, casting a glance across. "You ok?" His hand moves from my knee and grasps my hand in his. He strokes my palm with his fingertips.

"I'm so screwed up. Shit, Sebastian what am I going to do? I hate him." I look at him for guidance, but he stares at the road, his expression unreadable.

"You know you've always got a safe place to stay at Penmorrow. You and the children." He looks at me briefly again.

"That's so thoughtful, thank you." I squeeze his hand, with the realisation that I've misjudged this man, who is caring rather than arrogant.

"I mean it, Elizabeth. Whatever you need, I'm here for you."

"I know you do," I say gratefully, "and you've no idea how much that means to me, but this is something I have to work out by myself. I've made my bed and now I have to lie in it … that's what mum always says."

Sebastian parks in a space near to my office and cuts the engine. For a few moments we don't speak, my thoughts centred on the ramifications of today. He gets out of the car and walks around the car to open my door. He holds out a hand and I take it in mine and step from the car onto the pavement. For a fleeting moment, I feel a spark from his touch until he pulls his hand away and in that moment I know that I can't see Sebastian again ... not until I know for sure that Alan and I are over. The pain from this decision is tangible, a hard twisted knot forms in my stomach.

"Elizabeth, take my card," he says, handing me a small white card with his name and contact details embossed in gold.

"I want you to call me tonight when you get home, to let me know that you're ok."

"Actually Sebastian I'd rather not call. I need some space to think about my life, and to see if Alan and I can work through our problems," I tell him sorrowfully. Of course this isn't what I want. I want Sebastian - need to see him and *more*, but I am thinking now about the harsh reality and implications for my children, and the devastation they would feel if Alan and I were to separate.

"I see, as you wish of course. You have my card, and I'm here if you need me." He looks forlorn as he embraces me and kisses my hair. As he gets into his car and drives away without a backward glance, I want to run after his car – tell him I've made a mistake, I love him. Instead I walk with a heavy heart, back to work.

Ruth looks up from her desk as I enter our offices. She looks at my blotchy face and red rimmed eyes and frowns.

"Beth, love, whatever's happened?" She asks.

"Come and sit down and I'll make us a brew, you can tell me all about it."

"Oh Ruth, I've had the most amazing and the most *terrible* time" I whine. "I had lunch with the man who owns the house I went to last weekend and Alan must have followed us! He called me such dreadful names, Ruth and obviously thinks I've been having an affair."

"Blimey. You mean the Lord? What was he doing in Dorset?" she asks.

"Drove up just to see me."

"Hell, Beth I could tell you liked him. You're playing with fire you know. I warned you about something like this happening."

After a moment of contemplation, she asks what I intend to do. "I suggest you go home and talk to Alan before this 'thing' escalates."

"I know you're right, but it's made me realise I definitely don't want my life with Alan. I still want *more*, I want to feel desired and sexy and not just a drudge – I want to be *me* and but I've forgotten who *me* is!" I sob.

"I understand Beth, I really do," she replies. "Look, I know it's a cliché but the grass really isn't greener on the other side. Give it a month or two with the Lord and I guarantee he'll be farting, snoring and boring the pants off you just like all men! It's all sex and candlelight for the first few weeks and then wham! bam! Thank you mam! And before you know it you're washing his socks and wondering where the romance went. Trust me! We've talked about this before."

I look at Ruth incredulously, and we both burst into a giggling fit, hysteria rising within me once again. She has the most eloquent way of putting across her point and I do love her.

Ruth brings me a mug of tea, and I go to my office and close the door. There is so much to think about, but I'll face Alan later, for now I need to check my emails and catch up on some work. I wake up my laptop and sign in to my Yahoo account. Immediately I see an email from Alan's best friend, Mike. He was Best Man at our wedding and has known Alan since school days.

From: Mike Breeze<mlibreeze1043@hotmail.com>

To: Beth Dove

Sent: Friday 16 November 15:46

Subject: Alan

Hi Beth

I've had a call from Alan and he's in bits, love. I'm not sure what's going on with you but, honestly, I've not heard him so cut up before. He's asked me to talk some sense into you but you're a big girl, just don't hurt him.

Love Mike x

Mike has always taken Alan's side but then he would, he's his best friend. I decide not to answer his email, there being little point. Instead I pick up my things and set off for home, I really cannot concentrate on work. My head is full of hot kisses and angry husbands.

Alan's car is parked on the drive, so I know he didn't go back to work this afternoon. Letting myself into the house and closing the front door, I see Alan sat at the kitchen table clasping a tumbler of whisky. He's been drinking, that's not good.

"Alan, we need to talk." I sit down at the kitchen table across from him rather than next to him, wanting to put space between us. He looks at me over the top of his glass, which I note is nearly empty. "I know it looked bad today, but there's nothing going on," I continue.

"The kids are fine, nice of you to remember you have them." He's full of malice. I reach across and pick up his whisky tumbler, draining the glass. The amber liquid burns my throat, the alcohol fuelling my confidence.

"Do you know what Beth? What saddens me most is that if it's not him it'll be someone else. I don't make you happy and there's naff all I can do about it. I am who I am, and it's never going to be enough for you." He looks my in the eye and adds "I just don't like the bloody deceit Beth."

"You have to believe me Alan, it was just

lunch. I've got enough going on in my life without all this mess. Let's just get on with our lives as best we can for the kids ok?"

He nods dejectedly and I can see that he's weary, and drunk. I'm surprised, however, to get off so lightly after this afternoon's confrontation. I'm relieved but deep down, I know that I want to see Sebastian again – the deep longing in the pit of my stomach is gnawing away at my insides.

I go to bed early and open a book, and lose myself in the erotic fiction. As I read, I become the heroine and Sebastian is the lead male. It's me bending over the bed, and it's Sebastian who is pounding into me from behind. As I read on, my hand moves down between my legs and my fingers probe my wetness. I circle my sweetest bud with my finger with increasing urgency, and feel myself building, climbing to the release I need.

Drifting into a restless sleep, I'm back in the house in Cornwall. I'm running desperately from room to room and Sebastian is chasing me. He's dressed in black and is followed by the girl. They're covered in cobwebs, and screaming for me to run to the cellar. I wake up with a jolt, bathed in sweat.

6

Saturday dawns upon a beautiful crisp autumn day. Despite the frostiness from Alan throughout the rest of the week, I am determined to make the weekend an enjoyable one for the children. I have heard nothing further from Sebastian, nor from Simon.

Today, we have Alan's parents, Dora and Brian, his sister Sarah and her husband Nathan, and their young twin sons coming to lunch, so I have lots to do in preparation. It's usually an enjoyable time when the family visits, with lots of laughter although Nathan is a drinker, and a little unpredictable.

The roast lamb is ready and the family arrives, everyone is in good spirits and even Alan's mood has lifted. The twins are giggling as they jump on top of Joe, and Alan and Nathan are having a chatting in the study while Dora helps me in the kitchen. *Happy families*, I muse.

Lunch is delicious and the conversation, and wine, flows. Sarah tells us that she and Nathan are celebrating their forthcoming wedding anniversary next week, and Dora and Brian are babysitting so that they can have some 'couple' time.

Alan suggests a very good hotel where they may like to have dinner, *The Willows Hotel*. I shoot him a look, which says, "I hope you choke on your lamb," but he smirks back at me. It's apparent that he has already told Nathan about yesterday, as the two of them share knowing glances. Sarah, ever the diplomat, changes the subject but the digs keep coming from Alan throughout the rest of the meal. It ruins the day and, when the family departs at six, I am simmering with rage.

"You just couldn't bloody help yourself could you?" I hiss at him while I wash up the dishes.

"You humiliated me with all your sniping and made your family uncomfortable. Did you see Dora's face?"

"It's YOUR fault!" he hisses. "Don't you blame *me*. I've had just about enough of you. Why don't you bugger off with your Mr Range Rover, and leave me and my kids? You're never here anyway, you're always at work or up to God knows what…"

He's drunk again, and at this moment I hate him more than ever.

I need some space and so I grab my bag, car keys and jacket and open the front door, unsure as to where I am going, but needing to be alone.

Bella yells from the top of the stairs, "bloody nice one, mum. Piss off!" I turn to go to her, to tell her I am sorry that she heard her father and I arguing, but she is gone and I hear her door slam shut. Bereft, I leave the house.

I drive to the coast and park my car in the car park by West Way beach, it being a cold November evening the car park is nearly deserted. I decide to call Ruth and take out my phone from my bag. When I switch it on, I see there is a text message waiting for me.

Are you ok? S

Sebastian is so thoughtful, but he's disregarding my request for space and yet seems so intuitive to my needs. I forget about calling Ruth and instead text him back, well why not?

Things bad at home, thanks for caring X

His reply arrives almost immediately

I'm here if you need me

His message is brief, but the fact that he cares is comforting. Feeling better, I decide to head home but I erase his messages first.

Alan's watching television when I return home, and he ignores me. The children are very quiet, I presume that Joe also heard us arguing in the kitchen and I feel bad about that, I really do. Tomorrow will be a better day. This evening I will spend time with the kids and then take myself to bed and lose myself in the final chapters of my book. If only real life was like that book.

The week drags by incredibly slowly. As usual I'm running the children around to school, activities, parents' evening and of course working and each day seems more arduous than the previous one.

I haven't received any more messages from Sebastian despite constantly checking my phone. Thursday comes and I'm wading through reams of paperwork on my desk when my mobile phone rings. I don't recognize the number as I answer.

"Beth Dove speaking" I say.

"Elizabeth, it's Sebastian. Can you talk?"

My pulse races and I feel myself flushing, I didn't expect his call.

"Sebastian, how nice of you to call," my voice sounds just a tiny bit too high pitched and desperate.

"Are you alright?" he asks. So caring.

"Same old, same old," I reply. "My day just got a whole lot better with your call," I add cheekily.

"Glad to hear it. I've left you alone, as requested, but I'd like to see you." Technically he hasn't really left me alone as it's only been a few days since his text, but I'm flattered and relieved to hear his voice.

"I want you to come to stay at Penmorrow for a few days. It'll do you good." My stomach does a back flip as the enormity of what he is asking hits me. I would dearly love to go to Penmorrow and spend a few days in bed with Sebastian... I know that's not actually what he said but it is my interpretation.

"Sebastian, that would be wonderful but I can't. I have the children, work, not to mention how Alan would freak out." I am categorically saying no. It's the sensible thing to do. "Although, I could ask Mum if she'd have the kids for a couple of days. She knows how exhausted I am…" *Oh my willpower is staggering.*

"Good girl. Can you make the weekend or is Monday easier?" *my thoughtful Sebastian.*

"Let me call Mum, and text you back in a few minutes," the last of my self control dissipates, "and, Sebastian, I've missed you." I am a lost cause.

"I've missed you too. Call me back." He cuts the call.

I call my mother. "Mum, it's Beth, I hate to do this to you, but you know how stressed I've been lately. Things aren't good at home and work is manic, I'd be so grateful if you could please have the kids for the weekend for me? I thought I'd go to a spa for a rest." I hold my breath, ashamed that I'm lying to my own mother.

"Beth darling, is everything ok?" Intuitive mothers.

"Alan's being the same as usual. I wouldn't ask you but I really do need this," I tell her.

"Yes I can have them, of course I will, but on the condition that you go to a really nice spa and have a complete rest."

A rest. I'm not so sure that resting will be on our agenda. "Oh Mum, thank you so much. Yes, I plan to go to bed for two days and sleep. I'll drop the kids to you at 10am on Saturday."

We chat for a few more minutes and then I end the call. *What am I doing?* I wasn't being totally dishonest, I did indeed hope to spend two days in bed after all.

I text Sebastian, rather than call.

Mum said yes! I will be with you Sat pm. Can't wait and thank you. X

My phone pings as a reply is received.

You're texting – I said call. Plan on having fun.

He is so pedantic. *Plan on having fun?* That sounds so deliciously naughty.

Friday passes slowly and I can't wait for Saturday to come. I've told Alan that Mother suggested I take a short break in a spa, which is almost true, so that I can recharge my batteries. He actually agreed that this was a good idea but I can see that he doesn't trust me. However, he trusts my mother, and is satisfied that the children will be well looked after. I tell him that I will go from the spa directly to work on Monday and will be home that evening.

Saturday morning arrives and I rise early, and dress in a warm chocolate colour sweater dress and boots. I pack Bella and Joe's overnight bags and a small suitcase for myself, hiding my new underwear at the bottom of the case along with my favourite perfume and various clothing. I pack my swimsuit out of sudden panic as I am meant to be visiting a spa.

The kids are in the car and, after Alan bids me a curt goodbye, I drive to my mother's house. I kiss and hug my children and mother, feeling a pang of guilt as I do so. Then I am on my way and I haven't felt so excited since I was a teenager. I feel I may burst.

Penmorrow is even more spectacular than I remember. Perhaps because I won't be sharing it with countless other women, it seems even more inviting.

I drive slowly up the tree-lined drive and the butterflies in my tummy are doing back flips. I park and cut the engine and step from my car. As I take my small suitcase from the trunk, I inhale the salty sea air – it is invigorating and rejuvenating, and my troubles seem a million miles away. I hesitate at the imposing oak door of the austere house, before raising the lions' head and knocking loudly. Stepping back I expect to be greeted by Slave Girl, but instead Sebastian throws open the door. I hold my breath and look at this man and in that moment I want him more than I've ever wanted anyone or anything before.

7

We don't speak. Instead he takes me in his arms and hugs me tightly before kissing my hair. He smells so good, I breathe in his manly scent. Taking my suitcase from me, he takes my hand and leads me into the house. I hesitate in the hall but he has a firm, commanding grip on my hand. He puts my suitcase down next to the fireplace in the vast hall, and continues walking and I follow submissively.

Sebastian purposefully treads each stair, still gripping my hand he leads me up the Gothic looking staircase with cast-iron balustrade. We reach the top stair and he leads me to the left, underneath a vast octagonal lantern and down a long straight passageway off which are several closed doors. He stops at the fourth door on the left and turns the handle, pushing open the heavy oak door and I follow him.

Sebastian stops in the centre of the room and pulls me into his arms. All that I'm aware of is a vast four-poster bed with ornate carving and heavy, dark purple velour drapes.

We kiss then, our tongues hungrily seeking each other's. His lips bruise mine with his passion and I moan with desire, a warm trickle seeping from my sex. I feel his hand press into the small of my back and move downwards, where it grasps and kneads my buttocks. He takes a handful of my hair with his other hand and tugs it firmly. Still our tongues explore each other and I thread my fingers through the short hair at his nape, pulling on it, consumed with passion. He bites my lip and I wince but seek more hungrily.

I feel Sebastian unzipping my dress and, as he glides the zip down, my spine tingles. He slides it off each shoulder and it slithers to the floor. He unhooks my bra and I press my naked breasts against him, my nipples hardening painfully, elongating with the need for his touch. I pull back and lift his sweater over his head and he raises his arms to help me, then I take off his t-shirt and both are cast to the floor. He pulls me tightly to him and my nipples now press against his bare chest, the mass of dark hairs there tickling my skin. His muscles are well defined and hard as I trace my fingers across his bare chest. He is the most beautiful male specimen I have ever seen and I am feral with desire for him.

He runs his palms firmly down my back, his fingers finding purchase in the elastic of my panties, which he roughly pulls down over my hips, tapping at each leg to step out of them. Naked and squirming with desire, my juices coat my thighs as I yearn for his touch on my clit and his cock inside me, deep, oh so deep. Pushing my hips forward, I gyrate my groin against his hard cock, which is pressing through the denim of his jeans screaming to be released. I undo his leather belt and tug down his zipper, my impatience growing.

"Mmm so impatient Elizabeth. You need it darling, don't you…" he breathes.

A gasp escapes my lips as I take his huge, erect penis in my hand and squeeze it's length, rejoicing at the way it thickens in my hand. It's been such a very long time since I felt so desired, since I could be free to explore my own desires. ·I can't wait any longer.

He guides me backwards until I feel the hard frame of the bed against the backs of my thighs and then he pushes me hard, down onto the bed so that my ass is on the mattress, but my legs are draped over the frame. He bends and lifts each of my feet from the soft carpet, and I feel my legs lifted… so high and apart, exposing me, opening me wide to his scrutiny and will. He kneels then, placing my legs over each of his strong, broad shoulders.

Arching my back, I close my eyes and wait for what I know will come. His kisses trail moistly on the inside of my thighs. "Yes, oh yes, higher... go higher." He's driving me insane.

"If you tell me what to do, I'll stop Elizabeth."

What? Oh no, don't stop. Please.

He pauses a moment, to punctuate his point, before his fingers part my labia, the tip of his tongue brushing lightly at my clit. It's exquisite and I relish every flick, side to side, then circling as I throb down there. My fingers reach down, tugging at his hair, pulling his tongue harder onto me until the full roughness of his tongue is driving me wild, lapping again and again across my clit, circling until I feel my orgasm building. The warm flush builds from my pulsing sweet spot, and courses through my groin to my stomach, my nipples aching, the tremors rocking me, unrelenting. He licks clean my liquor, his tongue tracing a line from my pubis to my navel ... to each of my nipples and up to my neck then settles his lips on mine. His tender kiss deepens, the sweetness on his tongue coating mine, his mouth and chin drenched in my juices.

He moves away and lies next to me on the bed, as he does so he pulls me on top of him and I am looking down into his lustful eyes. He grabs a fistful of my hair again and I feel him pushing me down.

My lips leave the salty harbour of his neck, trailing pecked kisses over his heart … to a downward path that follows the line of his course black curls from taught stomach to his mound of thick manly pubic hair. His erection lengthens in my palm as he expels a hiss. "Yes. Take me in your mouth. Now." I need no encouragement; my tongue lapping the first bead of salty dew from the head of his cock as his manhood slips into my mouth. His hips buck with each teasing suck in hollowed cheek - taking him out and licking his crown, before welcoming his thrusts into open throat, my hand milking and stroking his shaft at its root. How he moans and writhes, guiding me with his strong grip.

"Yesss, that's right. Take it deep, good

girl". His hand is pushing my head down at a fast rhythmic pace until suddenly, he pulls me by my hair with a sharpness that draws a gasp. Maintaining the pressure on my hair, he forces me up toward him then releases his grip. "Ride me." Leveraging my hips he guides me into position then tugs me down to be speared by his slick crown. I am so very wet that he glides into me in spite of his girth. My vagina stretches, coating him in my new arousal yet his length is such that I gasp, struggling to take all of him into me. Grinding down hard, he fills me completely to my end and holds me firmly in place, my back arched, head thrown back as I moan in ecstasy.

I've waited so long for this and so I savour every delicious inch of him with a hunger that can't be sated. Leaning down, my hair tumbles in a curtain over my face as my mouth seeks his, sucking at his bottom lip through panted breaths. Up and down, he sets a gruelling pace - my orgasm building again as his hardness strikes my deep bundle of nerves. Our fingers lace in the air, his moans louder now as he chases his own climax. With a rasped cry, he explodes deep inside me as I too shatter onto him, my orgasm causing my whole body to shudder uncontrollably. Again he cries out, and it sounds like 'Libby' but it could be 'baby' - the sound is fleeting and I can't be sure. Exhausted, I flop down onto his chest, his breathing is laboured and he's hot and slick against my skin.

"Fuck, Elizabeth, you have real potential." *What the hell does that mean? Was I good or was I crap with the potential to be less crap?* I'll talk about that comment later but for now I love being in his arms, lying on top of him, my head nestled against his chest, listening to his heart beating strongly. He feels so powerful, so full of testosterone, a real man. *My man?* At this moment I'm glad that he chose me, none of the other 25 women but only *me*.

We doze peacefully and when I stir it's nearly nightfall. The light is fading fast and shadows cloak the room, rendering it rather eery. As I grow accustomed to the poor light,

I take in my surroundings. The room is huge despite the dark, heavy furniture. There is a vast, ornately carved armoire and matching eight-drawer chest upon which photographs sit in silver frames. A carved chaise upholstered in dark crimson silk, sits on ball and claw feet beneath the mullioned window. There is an enormous chest beside the door and a winged leather armchair is placed beside a wooden mantled fireplace. It's a manly room lacking a woman's feminine touch.

Sebastian stirs beside me and opens his eyes with a sleepy stretch and yawn before pulling me toward him and planting a kiss on my shoulder. "Come, let's go and eat, I'm ravenous," he says, climbing out of bed to retrieve his jeans from the tangled mess of clothes on the floor and tugging them on. Taking my hand he pulls me reluctantly from the bed. "There's a bathroom through there," he indicates to a door next to the armoire. "Freshen up and put on the robe behind the door. I'll be in the kitchen." Before I can answer he turns and leaves. He seems distant, dismissive almost and I feel the old feelings of self-doubt creep back. What we did was amazing and I want him to share the glow I feel. I feel so insecure yet know that the feeling is irrational. *I need to get a grip!*

The bathroom is vast and I wonder if it was originally another bedroom. 'Bedchamber' is what it would have been called in days gone by. The white enamelled bath sits proudly in the centre of the bathroom, upon grey marble floor tiles – its weight is supported by curved black wrought iron legs, with brass ball and claw feet fashioned in the same style as the chaise in the bedroom. I wonder if it is original or reproduction but it looks authentic so I assume that it is. There are modern touches, I notice, such as twin basins with glass shelves above each. On one shelf sits a variety of Sebastian's shaving equipment, aftershave and a comb. On the neighbouring shelf are a selection of female perfumes in glass bottles, Chanel and Christian Dior. There is a bone-handled hairbrush and a silver cased lipstick. I pull off the lid and twist, it is a bright blood red and I can see it's been used. The thought occurs to me that these may be Libby's perfume and cosmetics. I wonder if he is therefore keeping his dead wife's toiletries, and if so then it is certainly macabre. If not Libby's then which other woman could these belong to? Evidently it's a woman with whom Sebastian is intimate, or they wouldn't be in his private bathroom. This is another thing to quiz him about and the more I reflect, I wonder also if the silk robe hanging on a hook behind the door also belongs to the other woman.

The warm water cleanses my mind as well as my body. As instructed, I slip on the short black silk robe and tie the belt. It has a single red rose embroidered on the right breast and it feels luxurious and cool against my skin but a shiver travels down my spine as I ponder the provenance of it. Studying myself in the mirror, the flushed, sex-tousled haired woman I see staring back at me, is the woman who has been waiting to be freed for seventeen long years. I blow the vamp a kiss in the mirror and head downstairs to find Sebastian.

A delicious smell greets me when I walk into the kitchen and I realise that I am ravenous. Sebastian towers over the range, stirring something in a heavy copper pan; I drop a kiss on the back of his neck, my arms encircling his narrow hips as I peer into the pan to see what he is cooking.

"Hope you're hungry, Elizabeth, I make a mean bolognaise sauce!"

"Mmm, it smells yummy and I'm starving. I can't think why!" I wink at him and he returns a sexy wry smile.

"Sit" he gestures, with his wooden spoon, to the church pew and I take a seat. The candle is lit and it casts a warm golden glow across the chunky wooden table. I sit and watch him moving deftly about the kitchen preparing our food with a relaxed competence. He pours me a large glass of mellow red wine of which I take a deep drink, enjoying the warm flush from the alcohol as I watch Sebastian work. Setting two dishes of spaghetti bolognaise, spoons and forks on the table, he nudges a small dish of Parmesan shavings toward me.

"You're such a good cook, Sebastian," I flatter him and I mean it as I slide a dish of the tempting food to my place setting and take some Parmesan. "Do you cook for yourself every day?"

"No, I enjoy cooking occasionally, but Scarlett cooks for me. She prepared the meal for the Business event. She's exceptional, very capable ... and imaginative." *Wait right there, fella. Are we talking about cooking, or something else?* I bite my lip.

"I just bet she is!" I retort without subtlety, but resentment creeps up on me from nowhere.

Sebastian puts down his cutlery and frowns at me. "Elizabeth Dove, are you jealous?" he asks, all innocence and boyish charm.

"Should I be?" I retort, shovelling a forkful of bolognaise into my mouth nonchalantly, my eyes firmly locked onto my food.

"I don't tolerate jealousy Elizabeth, I've already told you I like to surround myself with beautiful things."

I sulk into my pasta, aware that his eyes are focused on me. "I'm not the jealous type Sebastian, I just find it weird that you have a beautiful woman living here … just you and her. Where does she sleep? Does she have staff quarters?"

"I know what you're implying Elizabeth, and I don't like it. Scarlett works for me, do you understand? And yes, she has her own quarters downstairs." He looks annoyed but, me being me, I persevere.

"Downstairs? In a cellar?" I ask incredulously.

"The cellar, Elizabeth, is probably twice the square footage of your entire house." He replies arrogantly.

"There's an entire network of rooms below us which used to serve as the working hub of this house. I'll show you tomorrow."

"I look forward to that," I say, with trepidation. "While we're on the subject Sebastian, who do the perfume, cosmetics and this robe belong to?" I tug nervously at my robe and regard him with suspicion.

His dark brows are set in a frown, his lips a stern line and the tension between us is now tangible. "They belong to you. Whom did you presume they belonged to? I bought them for you. Scarlett chose them actually. Frankly, I'm growing tired of your insecurity. Eat."

"I'm not hungry," I pout, my appetite suppressed at the thought of Slave Girl choosing something so intimate for me.

"You'll need the energy, I plan to keep you on the go all night. Now do as you're told. Eat." He's determined and obstreperous. With a petulant sigh I push my food around the bowl, managing to swallow a few mouthfuls of the steaming minced beef. He regards me sternly as he eats his food. I'm learning that Sebastian can be stubborn, evasive and dark. Not qualities I am familiar with or particularly fond of.

Glancing at the wooden clock, hanging by a short rope from an iron meat hook above the range, it's surprising that it's already nearly eight o'clock. I must call the children and say goodnight to them. I push my bowl aside.

"I've got to call the children, won't be long."

"Sure, go ahead," he says.

I take my bowl to the sink and leave the kitchen, still feeling moody. In the hallway I retrieve my phone from my bag and speed dial my mother's number. She's pleased that I call and asks me how I'm enjoying the spa. *Very relaxing,* I lie. I tell her that I've spent several hours in bed and have just eaten dinner, and she's pleased to hear this. I feel very guilty then.

Joe comes on the line and babbles about Grandma's house and lists the junk food she has fed him and I ask to speak with Bella. Typically moody, Bella has little to say and is eager to get back to a vampire series she's watching. It feels good to talk to them in spite of the shame I feel at the deceit. I end the call with several kisses and 'goodnights' and a deep longing to hold my children and smell their freshly washed hair.

Replacing my phone in my bag, I feel melancholy. When I turn Sebastian is leaning against the wall, watching me. I presume he has listened to my conversation, which I find overtly intrusive. He cocks his eyebrow and regards me with an expression that is hard to read. "Lying comes quite easily to you it seems, Elizabeth." His eyes are dark and smouldering. "You have the makings of a bad girl. I like that."

I bet you do, you weirdo, I think. *My weirdo.*

"I have a gift for you, come here," he commands.

"For me?" I'm intrigued - I love gifts but rarely receive them. I go to him, eager to receive my gift.

"Turn around." I do as I'm told and turn my back to him. He moves my long blonde hair away from my neck and I feel a cool cord being slipped around my throat. Fear creeps upon me but then Sebastian fixes a clasp behind my neck and turns me around to face him. My hands go to my throat and touch a fine silky choker with a bead decoration to the front. His expression has changed, jaw tensed he stares at the choker and then his eyes lock on mine with a faraway look that I haven't seen before. "You're beautiful," he whispers hoarsely.

"Sebastian … thank you," I rock onto my toes and kiss his full, sculpted masculine mouth with a gratitude that is heartfelt. He closes his eyes and inhales deeply as my lips leave his.

"Come and look." He leads me by the hand to the ornate gilded mirror above the fireplace in the hall and I gaze upon the choker. It is the finest black ribbon, in the centre is a tiny, sparkling diamond surrounded by a cluster of smaller diamonds. It's exquisite and I gasp as my fingers gently feel the silkiness of the ribbon and the roughness of the diamonds.

"I can't accept this Sebastian it's too beautiful, simply stunning." A fervent kiss to my neck silences me and I lean back against him.

"You *will* accept it, in fact I insist that you wear it when you're with me here. It's a symbol that you are mine."

Something stirs in me and I try to recall where I have seen a similar choker recently but I can't remember. I love it – it's sexy, beautiful and it's Sebastian's gift to me so I will treasure it. Of course I won't be able to wear it other than with him anyway, Alan really would have something to say about this. "Yes. I'm yours," I reply. "Oh, Sebastian I love it, thank you so very much." I'm grinning and feel happier than I have in a long time.

"You're very welcome, you deserve to have beautiful things Elizabeth. You're a very beautiful woman. I don't think you realise just how incredible you are." My lips find his and we share a lingering kiss.

"Come with me, I want to show you something," he says and I follow him into his study. An oversized antique desk sits against the far wall and to either side are three drawers. He pulls open the top drawer and pulls out a large, blue leather bound book, lifting the cover open he reveals that it's a photograph album. "Sit down." He pulls forward a dark green, leather button backed chair and I sit forward, eager to see the photos. "You asked about my family, well here they are."

Looking at the first page I see three black and white photos of an elegant couple and a small boy. In the first, the couple strike a formal pose – the woman is seated and she cradles a baby dressed in a long white gown, the man stands stiffly to the right and slightly behind, and has a hand placed on the woman's shoulder. The second photograph seems to have been taken at the same sitting but this time the couple are sat side by side and the man holds the infant. The woman is smiling in both photographs but the man looks stern, stuffy. The third photograph is far more relaxed, the woman seated casually on a picnic rug with a baby who is barely old enough to sit up resting against her legs. "Are these your parents? Is this you?" I ask, secretly delighted that he's finally sharing part of himself with me.

"Yes, my mother, father and I. Those two were taken on the day of my baptism. The other was taken at Penmorrow. We used to picnic up by the old oak," he replied.

"You were adorable!" I exclaim. "Such a gorgeous chubby little baby."

Sebastian chuckles, turns the page and I see that the young Sebastian is approximately three years old in the single photograph. He is stood next to an elderly, frail looking lady and is petting a large golden retriever dog, which I presume may have been a hunting dog.

"Your Grandma?" I ask.

"Yes. My Grandmother, Mary, was sick

when that photo was taken but she lasted another three years before she died. I loved her. I remember how she used to sit with me by the fire in the Great Hall and tell me stories about the old days at Penmorrow … the parties she and Grandfather held. I think things were very different in her day. There were certainly more staff living and working on the estate. They used to hold shooting parties, and at the time kept a kennel of twelve beagles. I recall being scared of those gun dogs because they seemed always to be barking, and I remember seeing them fed with pieces of raw meat which the kennel hand told me was pieces of naughty boys. Here, this is me when I graduated." He flicks through several pages and shows me a photograph of a fresh-faced young man in mortarboard hat and gown clutching a scroll.

"Handsome and clever," I tease and he smacks my behind playfully, sending a tug to my core. "So where are your mum and dad now?" I ask.

"They both died. They were both in their

forties when they had me. Mother died when she was sixty-two of breast cancer, and my father five years ago after a stroke. That's when I inherited this old pile and my title. Unfortunately with no heir, it's likely this place will go to my cousin and then my nephew who both live in Australia. I'm sure they'll sell it. Father would turn in his grave if that were to happen."

"Oh, Sebastian that would break your heart."

"Things change, Elizabeth," he shrugs with a frown. He seems melancholy and reflective, as though the historical weight and expectations of generations of De Montforts, rest squarely on his shoulders. I understand now what he meant by responsibility and burden, and my heart aches for my poor Sebastian, who is alone and with the weight of the world upon his shoulders.

"So, you and Libby didn't want children?"

He seems to blanch at that question. Poor Libby seems a taboo subject.

"We tried, but she … had problems. Not physical problems. Mental health problems, and she was always having one treatment or another and children just didn't happen for us."

I feel sad for him, for both of them, but I wonder what kind of mental health problems she suffered from. "Was it depression?" I ask tenderly.

"Depression and a whole bunch of other stuff. I don't want to talk about it." He closes the album and I regret pushing him about Libby. "Anyway, enough of this, BED!" He playfully pats my ass. A flutter of excitement runs through me, I hope he doesn't mean sleep.

Sebastian turns out the downstairs lights and I follow him up to his bedroom, it's an eerie house, I wonder if it is haunted and shiver at the thought. Closing the bedroom door, he turns on the small nightstand lamps, giving an intimate feel to the room. He pulls at the tie of my robe and it falls open, exposing my nakedness and I feel suddenly overtly aware of my body and its blemishes and imperfections. Even after what we did earlier, I'm not used to intimacy or showing my body but at the same time I yearn to feel his touch again. He slips my robe from my shoulders and now I am naked except for the choker around my throat, I do feel sexy for the first time in years. Not cheap or dirty but desired and feminine.

He stands behind me, his arms encircling my waist. Sweeping my hair over my right shoulder he kisses the nape of my neck, his arousal pressing hard against my sacrum. My breath catches, nipples harden and my heart beat quickens at his touch. "Close your eyes." He moves away from me, then returns and I feel silky fabric placed over my eyes and tied at the back of my head – *Oh goodness!* He's blindfolded me. This is so erotic and a first for me. He guides me to the edge of the bed. "I want you to lie down on your back Elizabeth, you have to trust me, whatever I do to you is for your pleasure as well as mine okay?" I have no idea what he's going to do to me but right now he can do what he wants, this is so exciting. I do as I'm told and lie back on the bed in total darkness.

"Open your legs," he commands.

Compliantly, I move my legs apart, feeling exposed and vulnerable yet creamy with desire. I hear him moving in the room but I can't see him. This is beyond erotic. I feel something soft and light tickling the sole of my left foot and then my right, a giggle escapes my lips. The tickle stops, I fall silent. The tickling sensation travels slowly across the tops of my feet, up my shins, to my knees. It moves to the inside of my legs and travels up toward my thighs. It's unbelievably arousing and soon the light tickle arrives at my sweet spot. I know now that he's using a feather and as it whispers over my clit again and again, I cry out but it's unrelenting. The sensation and anticipation increase until the raw and feral need for gratification becomes unendurable.

"More. Give me more. I need to come," I pant demandingly.

"No. Not yet." He stops abruptly, until my ebb subsides, before teasing again and again with this insufferable torture, and I'm desperate for release. The tickling stops and the room is silent. Frustration overcomes me.

"Dammit Sebastian. Stop teasing me," I cry.

"Patience. You come when I allow you to come." I hear a drawer open and close, I reach for the blindfold but a firm hand clasps mine and stops me.

"Trust me," he whispers in my ear. "This will be incredible for you." Cold metal touches my nipple and I jerk away from it. The metal flicks over my other nipple, which is hard and waiting.

"What the hell is that?" I demand.

"Sshh. Enjoy the sensation." The coldness is gone from my nipples. I wait, panting. Every fibre, every nerve ending awaits the next sensation. When it touches me once more, it's on my thigh. The coldness drags slowly up each thigh in turn, before pressing hard against my pussy. Pushing harder now, the cool phallus struggles to enter me, it's too large. I'm frantic, arching my back to aid the passage so that I can be filled, and it's inside me. Gloriously hard, it's thrust further until the pain almost overwhelms the pleasure. He rotates it and repeatedly drives it against my G spot, and I scream for him to stop, lest I climax without his permission.

"Come for me now. That's right, feel it, baby," he instructs and I abandon all control as the orgasm courses through my body in waves that don't subside. The tremors continue until he slides the thing out of me, only then does my body settle. He removes the blindfold and kisses me but I'm spent and confused.

"That was just for you, Elizabeth, but this is just for me now." He turns me over roughly, pulls me onto my hands and knees, and slaps my raised bare buttock with the flat of his hand, so hard that it stings and I cry out in surprised protestation. Then he's kissing my smarting skin, before holding fast to my hips and pounding into me hard. He pistons into me, faster and deeper , his testicles thwacking against me, until he reaches his own throbbing climax, collapsing over my arched back as he finds his release.

As we lie side by side in a comfortable silence, I begin to dwell on the confusion in my mind. On one hand, I've just had the most amazing sex but, conversely, his roughness, and memories of my afternoon with Simon are awakened. The roughness is so erotic, and again, I feel ashamed that I enjoyed the sting of his hand. I have so much to consider, such a disparity between my real life and my experience here at Penmorrow with Sebastian.

"So deep in thought my love," he traces his lips across my shoulder and pulls me into his embrace.

"What was that?" I croak.

"This?" he reaches over the side of the bed, and scoops up the object of my torture from the floor. He rests on one elbow as he holds it out to me. I take it and feel the weight in my hands - it's heavy and cool in a matt silver finish. Cone shaped, it is wide at the base and tapers to a rounded point and is so enormous, that I need two hands to hold it.

"Holy crap, Sebastian." Wide eyed I pass the thing back to him. He drops it to the floor with a loud thud. "That was too bloody much," I'm angry.

"Yes, I agree," he says. "But that was the hardest you've ever come, wasn't it Elizabeth?"

"Well, yes. But the way you teased me, I was going out of my mind Sebastian."

"It's part of my dynamic. By denying and then allowing you an orgasm, it's so much more intense when it comes. For you and me. From now on," he whispers against my ear, "you only come when I give you permission. I own your orgasms. Understood?" He kisses my earlobe.

I sit up, *ouch I'm sore,* and slap his shoulder.

He laughs! "Good shot!" A smirk curves his mouth, he swipes away my hand as it rises to strike him again.

"Who the hell do you think you are?" I yell, really mad now.

"Go with it, darling. You know you want to." He pushes me back against the pillows and tickles me while I fight to push him off. He's too strong for me and soon I'm laughing and giggling when I want to be furious with him.

"Go to sleep Elizabeth, we'll talk about it all tomorrow. I want to show you the grounds and more of the house tomorrow too."

"Night Sebastian, you infuriating, weird, twisted man," I murmur drowsily as sleep envelopes me in her grey cloak.

I'm running through the house and it is dark, so unnervingly gloomy. I can't look back, I have to get out but a woman dressed in black is gaining on me.

Her face is white — almost translucent — and she's screaming at me, "he's mine. You must die."

I slam into furniture, throw it aside, I have got to escape, she's coming, she's coming...oh so near now... MY GOD...MY GOD...NO DON'T...

8

The sense of panic consumes me; eyes snap open, sweat beads my top lip. Where am I?

"Hush, you had a nightmare darling. It's ok you're safe, you're here with me in bed... it's all over Elizabeth" he soothes.

My vision begins to clear, but the face of the woman in black haunts me still. I shudder and sit up, turning on the lamp on the nightstand. Blinking, my eyes adjust to the light and all is as it should be and so I start to calm down. Sebastian is stroking my back, and yet I can't shake off a feeling of foreboding. Folding me in his safe embrace, we nestle under the covers together until a more peaceful sleep eventually comes.

After a fitful night, the morning brings a languid start to the day. Sebastian brings mugs of coffee and we sit up against our feather filled pillows, drinking and chatting easily and I welcome the domesticity.

"Hungry?" asks Sebastian.

"Ravenous" I reply.

He lifts his eyebrow and I know that wicked glint in his eye.

"For food. I'm hungry for food," I laugh.

We are soon washed and dressed and making our way downstairs. On reaching the hall I stop to retrieve my phone from my bag while Sebastian continues to the kitchen. I text my mother, telling her that I'm fine, to kiss the children for me, I'm missing them all. There are no messages from Alan and I make a mental note to text him later, guilt besieging me.

In the kitchen the hired help is cracking eggs into a bowl, I recognise her as the woman to whom I gave my business card previously. She smiles at me as I enter, but her smile seems disingenuous. The hairs prick on the back of my neck as realisation dawns on me that hers is the face of the woman in my nightmare.

Don't be ridiculous, Beth. She was on your mind, that's all.

"You must be Scarlett," I say with a cheeriness I don't feel. "We haven't really been introduced." I hold out my hand and she shakes it lightly and returns to the eggs. She's dressed in the black slim fitting dress again I observe, and then I freeze. She's wearing a black choker around her slim throat. Walking nearer to her so that I can look more closely, it's apparent that her band isn't adorned with diamonds but even so, it denotes the same amatory look as mine. Rage and resentment simmer inside me with the realisation that Sebastian dresses his 'staff' as he does his lover. It's bizarre and in my opinion, unacceptable.

As I sit down on the hard pew opposite Sebastian, my mind tries to make sense of the relationship between them. Seeing her this morning, domestic Goddess in his kitchen cooking breakfast, sharing the intimacy of his gift, just confirms my suspicions about their relationship and a knot deep in my belly tightens with the apparent affirmation that I'm sharing my perfect man. I feel used and stupid.

Sebastian is studying me and when I look at him, he has a quizzical look on his face. He's presumably detected my sudden change in mood. "Everything okay?" he asks me.

"Fine. I'm just not hungry suddenly," I say resolutely, as a plate of scrambled eggs and bacon is placed before me.

"Eat Elizabeth, then we'll go for a walk." He cannot command me, I'm not one of his salaried harlots and I shoot him a frosty glare.

"I'm not a child, Sebastian," I rebuke. "If

I'm not hungry then I won't eat." Sliding the plate away from me, I sit defiantly with arms folded across my chest daring him, with my stare, to push the point further.

"Very well Elizabeth, we'll discuss this later. Scarlett, fetch our coats." He barks his order to the girl, and I see how she immediately does as he bids.

"Yes Sir." Scarlett leaves the kitchen to fetch our coats.

"You'll learn I hope, Elizabeth, that when I ask you to do something it's for your own good. By defying me you haven't achieved anything other than to be very hungry and to make me cross."

I stare at him, perplexed. He's the most infuriating person and yet his imposing manner is appealing, masculine, and contrasts so distinctly to Alan.

Scarlett returns to the kitchen and passes each of us our coat, which we shrug on. Dressed for the cold winter morning we leave the warmth of Penmorrow and I prepare myself for the confrontation that seems inevitable.

The cold salty air is bracing and our cheeks blanche from the biting wind. Sebastian proffers a hand, which I take in mine reluctantly, and leads me across the formal gardens and through a wooded area beyond. The trees break to reveal a spectacular rocky precipice and dramatic seascape ahead. We are prevented from nearing the cliff edge by a high barbed wire fence. Standing side by side, we don't speak as we take in the view of the inky blue sea with foaming surf, below.

He breaks the silence, "why do you stay with Alan?" I don't reply but he continues, "It's quite obvious that you aren't happy."

"I can't afford to go it alone. The business is doing ok, but if we don't expand soon we'll get left behind and competitors will force us out of business. He doesn't earn much but it keeps us going financially. Mainly though, it's the children keeping us together. If you had kids you'd understand," I snap. I know immediately that it was a cruel thing to say and I squeeze Sebastian's hand, glancing at him and noting with regret his hurt expression.

"I'm sorry, that was mean. I know you wanted children, what I meant to say was there's an enormous pressure to play 'happy families,' when you have kids they become your sole focus, or *should* do." I realise as I'm speaking, that I'm not exactly putting my children foremost by being here with Sebastian, leaving my husband and children at home and basing my absence on a lie.

"I'm not a father, as you point out, but I should think that your children are astute. I imagine that they hear arguments or certainly pick up on the negativity between you?"

He has a valid point. Alan and I often forget the children are within earshot when we fight, it's so easy to be entirely wrapped up in ones' own world and not see the impact it has on others. "He used to make me happy, when we first met," I reflect, "but we've grown apart over the years… I guess our differences just became more evident. I feel … I want more. I want him to be assertive, for once I'd like *him* to take the lead, make decisions … man up and grow a pair!"

"And if he did that, Elizabeth, would he make you happy? Fulfilled? Or would you still want more? From what I sense, he can't give you what you need."

"And can *you* really give me what I need?" I ask shrilly. "Because from what I've seen in your house, you are the very last person to give me advice on relationships, mister."

He looks startled and takes my hand in his. "Whatever's gotten into you this morning?"

I pull away and thrust my hands in the deep pockets of my coat. "I'm just so confused," I tell him. "I feel like you and I have something… special, but then you go and do things that make me feel cheap. It's not normal, Sebastian. Not normal to do what you did to me last night. Not normal to give an employee the same sensual choker you gave to me."

"I see." His dark eyes regard me icily and the coldness sends a shiver through me, I pull my coat more tightly around me but it offers little warmth against the chill within.

"It doesn't mean anything … she doesn't mean anything," he garbles. "You're overthinking things, Elizabeth. Look, we're getting to know each other and that takes time and patience. You've got to realise, I *know* what you need and you've got to trust me on that." He takes my hand again and this time I don't pull away.

"And what would that be, Sebastian?"

"You need a dominant man, Elizabeth, one who'll tell you what you need to do, in all things. That isn't something Alan can give you, it's not in his nature from what you've told me about him. Not all men are assertive. They rely on their wives as though they are a replacement mother. Men, like me, are born to dominate. We know what we want and how to get it but we also know what women want and we give it to them, Elizabeth."

"It sounds more like control. Is that what this is about?" I ask weakly.

"Control yes. I need to be in control and if you don't relinquish control to me, I can't help you. You'll drift along. Stressed. Unhappy. Don't settle for less."

I shudder, not just because of the bracing wind whipping across the sea and lashing at our coats; my emotions are stirred by Sebastian's words, which are so incisive and to which I relate so wholly. "Well, we *are* still married, so I have to make the best of it. Come on. It's freezing, show me Penmorrow? I'm dying to look around." I take his hand in mine and we walk back toward the house, taking a different route so that he can show me the walled garden, maze and the old oak where he used to picnic as a child.

The grounds are beautiful, with the backdrop of the cliff and ocean, it's the most remarkable place I have ever been and I feel a belonging here. *If only my life had turned out differently, I could be happy here. I can change Sebastian.*

We explore the house, there are four formal rooms including the great [dining] hall, study, morning room and library. All are opulent in their own way, in spite of the tapestries looking faded, objet d'art being slightly dusty, there is an ageless charm, which has seen countless generations living amongst these rooms. My mood lifts and the awkwardness of before is forgotten as Sebastian delights in showing off his splendid home. He's like a young boy, animatedly detailing the provenance of his belongings and the history of his ancestors.

I squeal like a child when Sebastian shows me a hidden passageway, concealed by a false bookshelf in his study. I can barely contain my excitement, when the heavy door, disguised with painted books, heaves forth. He flicks a light switch on the wall above the first step, takes my hand and leads me through the secret doorway.

"This is unreal," I gush. "So these big old houses really do have secret passageways, I thought that was just in movies and books. This is so cool."

"Rumour has it, there is a tunnel somewhere under the house, leading to the cliffs, which used to be used by smugglers. They'd haul their loot and ill-gotten gains from small boats and stash it in the cellars, so folklore says."

"Wow. Real smugglers," I am enthralled by the romanticism of his tale.

The steps lead down and curve round out of sight, worn down in the middle of each tread as if Sebastian's servants or ancestors, or smugglers, have been sneaking around via this passage for centuries. I am guarded in case I brush cobwebs, as an arachnophobic, my eyes dart from side to side above my head as I gingerly take each step behind Sebastian, gripping firmly to the rope handrail. Curiously, there are no cobwebs, the steps look to be free of the dust and debris I expect to see and the walls and ceilings are thankfully missing the spiders I anticipate, clearly this staircase is in regular use.

We continue downward and to the left of the narrow stairwell, the light becoming dimmer now, my bravery receding as the gloominess encompasses. As we reach the final step, Sebastian flicks another switch and the way ahead is illuminated by the bulb hanging from the coarse, grey ceiling of the long corridor before us. The walls are arched and we walk on seemingly ancient flagstones. Sebastian walks without hesitancy, as though he frequents this passage and knows every inch as well as he knows his living quarters above us. I wonder where this leads.

"Is this where the servants would have worked?" I ask.

"Yes, this would have been a hive of activity years ago." He replies as he guides me through a low wooden doorway.

The room we enter is small, possibly eight

or nine square feet. To the right is a black wrought iron framed single bed, neatly made with crisp white sheets and a claret velvet throw folded precisely across the foot. To the left is a small washbasin, a dressing table with mirror and on the wall ahead, a wardrobe.

I walk over to the dressing table and pick up a half empty bottle of Chanel No.5 perfume, and I feel Sebastian move behind me. He reaches forward and takes the glass bottle from me removing the lid I feel a cool damp mist on my neck as he sprays the sensual fragrance on my skin. He doesn't touch or kiss me but instead he replaces the bottle on the table and leads me from the room.

"Whose room is that?" I probe, knowing that it is probably Scarlett's room and hating him for that. Jealousy is such a bitter pill.

"This is Scarlett's room," he confirms nonchalantly. He makes it sound so… normal but I cannot help but wonder what her job description, should one exist, comprise. Is it a prerequisite to share his bed, for example?

We continue along the passage and Sebastian shows me a further bedroom, comparable to Scarlett's room and a small utilitarian kitchen.

Soon, we enter a much larger room which appears to be a lounge; couches nestle against each wall and in the centre, covering the flagstones, lies a huge Persian rug in red, black and inky blue hues. My feet sink into the deep fibres - it's plush and luxurious pile too good for servants' quarters. There are two small wooden chests against one wall, upon which are table lamps; their bases are black, shiny naked female forms and each has a fringed red shade.

A silk robe lies strewn across the arm of a couch, and I glimpse the corner of a magazine protruding beneath it. I pick it up, staring at the glossy cover and am shocked to see a naked man and equally naked female. My eyes are drawn to the whip he is brandishing and the exposed female buttock waiting to be lashed. She wears a blindfold and is licking her blood red lips, as she appears to be pushing her hips back to meet the waiting blow.

"What the hell's this?" I am stunned, yet aroused enough to feel the burning in my sex.

"What do you think it is? Does it turn you on Elizabeth?" He smirks with a low growl.

"My point is, Sebastian, what the hell is Scarlett doing looking at porn in your home?" I ask incredulously, not yet diverting my gaze from the erotic picture.

"If you're so shocked why are you still looking at it?" Damn him. He is so infuriatingly right all the time. "It seems to me, Elizabeth, that you're fascinated by that image and…" he moves behind me, his hand reaches around my waist, down my midriff, inside the waistband of my grey woollen skirt, finds the waistband of my tights, his fingers forcing behind the snug elastic. His exploring fingers discover the top of my panties and push them down, aside, and his fingers travel down to my sex. I gasp as his middle finger slips between my labia, into my wetness. As he leans forward, into my back, his finger pushes deeper inside me and I push my hips forward to meet his finger, to take it deeper into me.

Moaning now, I close my eyes, lost in the glorious sensation as his finger now pulls out, finds my clit and slides and slips again and again over my sweet, throbbing, jewel.

"…and, yes, you *are* so turned on aren't you Elizabeth? Oh my God, you're dripping. That turns you on hmm?" Still his finger works on me, his other hand now underneath my cotton top, squeezing and pinching at my left nipple through my lace bra.

"You see the whip, darling? The way she wants it? The way she *wants* to be punished by him?"

"Sir! I'm so sorry!" The woman's voice snaps me out of my forbidden moment.

Sebastian withdraws his hand sharply and we spin around to face Scarlett. She is regarding us with a disdainful expression, as though she is disgusted to witness our passion and I feel suddenly ashamed. Smoothing down my clothes, conscious of my flushed face and dishevelled appearance, I force a smile and replace the magazine.

"Scarlett." He glares at her venomously.

"I'm sorry to have disturbed you both." She is looking at the magazine. "I'm sorry you found that. I should have put it away Sir, please forgive me." She is talking to Sebastian yet she doesn't catch his gaze instead looking down at her hands, which are nervously playing with the tie at the waist of her black dress.

"It's not your fault, we shouldn't be down here snooping," I try to reassure the girl who seems to be a bundle of nerves.

"I'm interrupting, I'll leave." She raises a perfectly plucked eyebrow and I see a smile play across her cherry red lips. She knows what I am. Adulterer.

The entire situation is making me feel uneasy again - the atmosphere between

Scarlett and 'Sir' is tense. I feel like an intruder and I'm consumed with the desire to get away from here. "I'll go, Sebastian," I mumble, looking past him, to the door. He grasps my arm roughly, a look of concern setting his mouth in a firm line and creasing his brow.

"NO, don't leave," there is hardness in his voice as he turns to face Scarlett. "Leave us…NOW! And next time you enter a room where I'm clearly with company, you don't interpose, do you understand?"

"Yes Sir, I…I'm sorry." She looks remorseful, chin down, as she turns and leaves the room.

"This is crazy," I tell him. "I feel like a spare prick in a whorehouse…literally!" my voice is full of venom and for a moment he looks aghast, then the coldness once again sets across his eyes, his hands ball into fists at his sides.

I run out of the room and into the gloomy passage, trying to recall which way we had come, I turn left. Disorientated now I slow to a fast walk but it doesn't look right – I don't pass the bedroom doors. I can here his heavy footsteps behind me.

"Elizabeth!" he calls, "come back, this is ridiculous."

I call back to him as I continue on my way, searching for something familiar, the staircase, "sorry Sebastian, it was a mistake coming here, I just need to get home."

Ahead of me is a dead end, just a dark wood arched doorway with iron latch blocks my passage. Looking back over my shoulder, I see that he's close. Reaching out, I press the latch and the ancient ironworks lifts, the door swinging open and I catch a brief glimpse of the room within. I see tools, lots of dark metal implements adorning the walls of what looks to be a cavernous cellar. As I strain my eyes to look more closely at the room, his hand thumps against the door and it slams shut.

"Don't go," he rasps. "You're

overreacting. Just calm down and come upstairs with me." He commands me as he commands Scarlett but he's intoxicating, edgy and the danger only exacerbates my excitement.

His study offers a welcome sanctuary and an air of normality again. We sit side by side on a leather love seat, and he takes my hand in his and rests it on his lap. His voice is earnest when he speaks. "Since Libby died, it's been so lonely here Elizabeth. Scarlett … supports me, she's my companion, she looks after me and keeps me sane."

"But if you have her… why do you need me?" I ask dejectedly. Suddenly I feel as though I don't belong anywhere; not with Alan, not here – I feel lost, cast adrift like a small boat drifting at sea.

"I *do* need you Elizabeth, more than you appreciate. I know you need me too, you don't realise it yet but you do. You have to trust me to know what you need, if you go back to him – to Alan – you'll never be happy." His finger gently tilts my chin so that

I'm looking into his eyes, such dark brooding eyes it's impossible to read his emotions.

"I know what you need." He does know me and right now he seems to be looking right into my soul.

"There's just so much... weirdness in this house," I say. "It's not normal Sebastian, to have that woman here – all sexy subservience. I don't understand why you want me when your needs are probably being met by... by her."

"I don't force her to stay, she's paid a decent wage, probably more than your staff earn. Yes she's attractive, but I told you I like to surround myself with beauty. It's nothing more than that. Trust me."

It sounds so lame to me now, when he says this. "Are you telling me she is nothing more to you than a maid?" I ask sceptically.

"There was a time when she was more. A very brief time," he confesses, his eyes hooded and his tone hushed. "I stopped that pretty quickly, but I think she'd like more."

"I see. Is that when you gave her the choker?"

"Yes. She chooses to wear it now, it's not something I've thought a great deal about, but I understand why it would upset you. I'll tell her to remove it."

"It's not just the bloody choker, Sebastian. Don't you see that?"

He runs a hand through his hair, his face pensive.

Looking at him, I question why I'm here. I seem to be adding more complication to my already overly complicated life, which was not my intention. "Look, Sebastian," I take his hand in mine, "I'm not sure why I'm here, what I was looking for, but… it's not me, this whole 'affair' charade isn't me. I've had the most amazing time, really, but now I want to get home and see the kids."

He looks crestfallen. His dark eyebrows knit into a frown, his eyes veiled with hurt and coldness, he pulls his hand away from my grasp. "You don't even comprehend what you need, and you're certainly kidding yourself if you think you can just go back to your *little* life in Dorset with Alan," he says malevolently. That confirms my decision to leave.

He stands on the stone steps to Penmorrow looking remorseful, like a scolded little boy. "Don't go."

"I have to, Sebastian. I'm so mixed up right now. I'll call you."

We embrace, and I leave. *Goodbye Sebastian.*

9

The journey home gives me sufficient time to reflect on the last twenty-four hours. The fact that I'm driving home a day earlier than planned is confirmation of the mistake I've made in staying with Sebastian, although I wonder how I will explain my early return to my mother and to Alan.

Fifty minutes into my journey, my phone bleeps to signal a text message and I pull into the next services to pee and to check the message. It is from Sebastian.

I wish you hadn't have left. Text me when home. S

Still no kiss I note, even after what we did together but I'm strangely relieved to receive his message, reassured that I haven't blown my relationship with him after all I said to him and leaving early as I did. Goodness knows why I care, he's clearly one screwed up cookie. *So am I though, we are both completely fucked up in our own ways.* I text back.

Leave me alone please, I need to sort things at home and don't need you complicating things for me x

His reply arrives even before I pull out of the service station onto the motorway.

Text me when home.

So bloody exasperating.

I arrive at my mother's house late in the afternoon. The dark winter evening is already threatening to close in and the stillness in the air signals the onset of the first frost of winter.

I park my car and walk up the familiar pathway to my mother's home. It has never been my home or somewhere I grew up so I feel no real attachment to this house, other than my mother lives here so it always holds a homely atmosphere and smells of mum's perfume and lavender soap.

Mum opens the door and ushers me in to the warmth of her home. "I wasn't expecting you until tomorrow dear, is everything ok?" she asks. So intuitive, she looks at my face and clutches me into her embrace as I crumble, sobbing on her shoulder.

"Sshh, whatever's the matter love?" she soothes. "Didn't you like the spa? Has something happened to Alan?"

Where do I begin? How do I tell her about my lies, my deceit, about Sebastian and his dark life? "Oh mum," I wail, "I've not been to a bloody spa." She looks confused but I continue, "I've been to stay with a man I met at a business event recently, oh God it's such a mess…I really like him but he's even more screwed up than me!" I exclaim.

"I'll make a brew, and you can tell me all about it. The kids are upstairs, so we won't be disturbed."

My mother sits me down and brings me a cup of hot sweet, milky tea – mum's answer to all crises, despite knowing I prefer coffee. We talk for quite some time about Sebastian but I am careful not to divulge any details about Scarlett or the porn. I just tell her that I realized that an affair is not for me. I love my kids too much to put them through a messy separation. She seems reassured that I'm not going to run away with this man and it's been good to talk and get these feelings out.

It's nearly nine o'clock when I pull in to our driveway with Joe and Bella. The lights are on in the front sitting room and I can see the silhouette of Alan watching television. Shutting the front door behind us, I call out to him that we're home. I think I hear a grumble from the sitting room in response, but it may have been the television. I hang my coat on the peg behind the front door and step into the room to see Alan. I'm eager to gauge his mood, as that will confirm whether or not he is suspicious of my whereabouts this past twenty-four hours. I need not have worried as he barely acknowledges me.

Joe still loves his bedtime chats and I welcome the return to normality. Kissing him goodnight, I turn out the light and check on Bella who is engrossed in Facebook, apparently chatting with a boy called Kyle and so I close her door and leave her to it.

In the sitting room, Alan's watching a documentary on quantum physics – frankly I'm amazed he understands the data presented although I suspect he's not paying attention to it. Sitting on the armchair next to him I try to concentrate on what the presenter is telling me but it's way over my head. I'm restless as thoughts of Penmorrow, cellars and Sebastian fill my mind until they become a jumbled cacophony of images. Looking at Alan, I can't comprehend how far removed his life is from Sebastian's and I resent my husband for his lack-lustre persona and meek disposition.

Alan picks up the remote control and presses the button to silence the television. Turning to me, I notice a flush in his cheeks and wonder if he's been drinking and I then I smell whisky. "Where the fuck have you been?" he spits. Astounded and panicky, I look wide-eyed at him and feign a look of innocence and surprise.

"At the spa Alan, where the hell do you think I've been?" I counter.

He laughs then, a deep, guttural belly laugh, which is not based on humour but some dark sense of irony. "You lying fucking bitch, I know you've not been to a bloody spa. I called every sodding spa on the south coast!" He takes a deep gulp of whisky from the crystal tumbler, which I see had been on the hearth next to his feet along with a near empty bottle. "What I don't bloody get," he continues, "is why you came back early – in fact, why you came back at all? If your life here is so bloody terrible, why don't you bugger off with whatshisname and do us all a favour?" The bitterness resonates through every word he spits at me. He looks so forlorn, downbeat and totally defeated as he looks at me now with contempt.

"Alan, I… I don't know what to say," my response is pathetic. I am a deer caught in the headlights knowing my fate but unable to change it. I know we're over but the guilt I feel, and bleakness of our marriage consumes me, and a tear winds it's way down my reddened cheek.

"Don't bloody say anything, I don't believe a word that comes out of your mouth. I've done everything I can to support you with your business, the kids, this house… I couldn't have done more…" He stares despondently into his empty tumbler.

"I know love," I reply, "we've just grown apart. We want different things out of life."

My phone bleeps in the kitchen - we both hear it, Alan huffs in irritation. "Probably lover boy, you'd better answer it." He reaches for the whisky bottle and drains the remaining alcohol into his glass, while I walk into the kitchen and take my phone from my handbag.

Presuming you're home now Elizabeth? You didn't call as I asked. S

I slip my phone into my pocket and retreat to the upstairs bathroom so that I can reply in private without antagonising Alan further.

Not replied as just got home, things awful here. Please don't text me, leave me alone!!

The phone whooshes as the message is sent and a sense of relief washes over me, with the knowledge that I have made the decision to end things with Sebastian, at least until such time as Alan and I have talked about our marriage and made rational decisions. I really don't need any more complications. Sitting on the edge of the bath, I stare at my phone screen, waiting for a reply from Sebastian, which doesn't come.

Downstairs, Alan has finished the bottle of whisky and is slurring his words. "So, watcha gonna do now that I know all aboutcha little love affair huh?" he's very drunk and there is little point continuing this discussion until he sobers up.

"Look Alan, why don't we get some rest and talk tomorrow. I'll finish work early and maybe the two of us can pop down to the Crown for a drink. Just the two of us, we can talk then?" I try to rationalise and calm him but can see the anger bubbling beneath the surface in my husband's face.

"Mum?" Joe has crept downstairs and is standing in the doorway looking anxious. "I heard Dad shouting." He looks at Alan, seeking reassurance that everything's alright, but we both look blankly at him unable to find words to reassure him.

Upstairs, Joe nestles down beneath his duvet and smiles at my goodnight kiss. Lying next to him on his narrow bed, I listen to his breathing settle as he falls asleep. Gazing at my sleeping son, I wonder what I'm going to do but then I hear Alan striding up the stairs. He throws open the door.

"I wanna talk to you...NOW!" he hisses. A sense of foreboding crawls through me, starting in the pit of my stomach.

"Downstairs" I whisper so as not to disturb Joe.

Alan is in the kitchen, pacing across the floor from the table to the sink, I can see the anger in his face and I suddenly feel afraid and unwilling to argue further tonight as I see his anger escalate. "What the hell's this?" He throws my mobile phone down onto the kitchen table and places his hands on his hips.

I pick up the phone, the screen is black and I raise my eyebrow questioningly. "It's my phone Alan, what's your problem?" I ask defiantly.

"The fucking 'problem' ish the messages on there." He is now very drunk and slurring his words. "Ish that *Him*, that tosser from the hotel you were with?" *Oh no, he's read my text messages.* Mentally slapping myself for not locking my phone with a passcode, I desperately think of an excuse to explain the texts but knowing that there is no plausible explanation I can proffer, I opt for the truth.

"It's not what you think, Alan," I try the gentle approach. "I've only seen him once since you saw us having lunch at the hotel. I stayed there last night..." Alan's eyes widen as the enormity of what I tell him sinks in, and I fear he is going to have a heart attack.

"How could you do this to us? What about the kids?" He is swaying now, his fury burning and the alcohol destabilising him. "What the fuck are you playing at?"

I start to cry through humiliation, guilt and genuine remorse at the distress I've caused my husband; this wasn't my intention. I had merely wanted to do something for *me* rather than for everyone else, to find myself - 'the real Beth Dove', whoever she now is.

"I don't know. I honestly don't. So...

where do we go from here?" my question seems superfluous now as it is evident Alan will not forgive me and so it seems inevitable now that we will separate.

"I'm outa here. Shit Beth you can do what you want, but I wanna see my kids…"

Sobbing, I go to him, try to hug him and he receives my embrace with an iron-rod back but to me, the hug is a farewell gesture and a shrug to our past, all tenderness is lost.

It doesn't take Alan long to throw a few clothes and toiletries into a suitcase. He's leaving me but before he goes, he kisses Joe's cheek as he sleeps, and whispers something to his slumbering son. Then he knocks on Bella's door. She removes her earphones as he enters her room and turns off her music, then I hear my daughter and husband talking in hushed voices. Shortly after, he leaves our home with a slam of the front door and I feel desolate.

I decide to go to bed – tomorrow I can

worry about what I'm going to do. Right now I feel exhausted.

10

On Monday morning Joe is quiet and pensive during the journey to school. Bella refused to travel with us, instead choosing to take the bus to school and there had been no point in arguing with her, she has her father's mulishness.

At nine o'clock I arrive at my office, business as usual. Ruth has her head buried in a stack of paperwork but looks up over her reading glasses as I arrive.

"Beth, how was your weekend? " she asks. I roll my eyes and sigh, giving her a look that says *'don't go there.'*

"Coffee, love, that's what you need, and then I want a full low-down on what you've been up to missy." she has never been the most diplomatic of my friends but she's the most determined, and so it will be that she will insist on a full account.

Over coffee, I tell Ruth about my fight with Alan and she listens sympathetically, without interrupting. When I have finished, she sighs heavily then gives me a tight hug.

"I'm so sorry you're going through this shit, Beth. He still won't go to couples counselling?"

"Not a hope, Ruth. God knows I've tried and tried. It feels like it's really over."

"I'm so sorry, love. So, if you didn't go to a spa, where *did* you go?"

I tell Ruth about my visit with Sebastian at Penmorrow. She is shocked and, I think, rather disappointed at my infidelity but that soon turns to curiosity, and she's now attempting to extract the finer details from me. "OK, so you've explained why you went and I kind of get that Beth, but tell me what happens now?   Are you going to see him again?"

"Absolutely NOT!" I exclaim.   "He's so complex, Ruth. He lives alone in that huge mansion… oh not entirely alone of course; he has a live-in housekeeper who is twenty-something, beautiful and sexy… and he tries to tell me that there's nothing going on any more, she is just staff but shit, she had an S&M magazine… When she caught us in the staff quarters, with the magazine, she looked at me as though *I* was intruding on her and Sebastian!"

"Whoa, slow down.   What do you mean 'any more' and S&M? You mean they *were* an item? And you mean the whole bondage thing?" she is enthralled and appalled in equal measure.

"Oh yes. Whips, the lot, and if she's in to that, and he clearly knew about it, then there has to be something strange going on there. He says they were fleetingly an item, but I'm not convinced.   I nearly forgot, he gave me the most beautiful choker." I lift my bag from the floor and fish around amongst the paraphernalia to retrieve the choker. I pass it to Ruth who studies it closely.

"Beth, it's rather sexy," Ruth admires the delicate ribbon and is evidently impressed by the sparkling diamond cluster. "Are these real?" She tilts the jewels toward the window and marvels as they sparkle.

"They're real, Ruth. Do you know what the bizarre thing is, though?" I don't wait for a reply, "Scarlett wears a choker too. Tell me that's not weird. They don't have diamonds, but it's the significance of the choker that worries me."

"That's weird, yep." She places the ribbon on the desk. "Beth, just don't complicate things any more than they are. Give yourself some space."

My phone bleeps. I snatch it from my bag and turn my back to Ruth as I open the message, which disappointingly is from Alan.

Staying with Mike. Will get Joe

Saturday at 11 and have him for the weekend. Bella can come too if she wants. Alan

"Shit. It's Alan," I tell Ruth. "He wants the children on Saturday, he's staying with Mike – you met him last year at the BBQ, he's a good friend to Alan so I'm glad he's staying with him." I'm also glad Alan hasn't done anything stupid. Mike will help him through this, which in turn, means my anxiety decreases.

"That's good, love. At least you know he's okay," she reassures me.

My phone bleeps again, I swipe my finger across the activating button and it wakes, revealing a message from Sebastian.

Will overlook your previous message Elizabeth. How are you? S

Will overlook my previous message? Such arrogance; this is a man who's evidently used to getting his own way. I reply to his text message, forgetting Ruth who is eying me inquisitively.

Sebastian, which part of 'leave me alone' do you not understand? B

'B' I simply signed myself as he does, without affection and laying bare my animosity toward him and his unwanted attention.

"Was that *him*?" asks Ruth, eyebrow cocked.

"Yes," I reply. "But I've made it very clear to him that it's over, I really don't need the hassle Ruth." I sound so sure and yet, deep inside me I long to be in his arms right at this moment. Dangerous thoughts. He replies swiftly.

Clearly you're upset. Meet me - we need to talk. I can help you, don't push me away. S

This floors me. He doesn't now 'fit' into the egotistical and insensible pigeonhole in which I've placed him. He wants to help me. "He wants to meet me, Ruth." I hand my phone to her and she glances over the thread of text messages.

"Be careful Beth. Men can be very manipulative and even more so when they spot vulnerability in a woman," she warns. "I know you well Beth, you will go to him and cry on his shoulder. Then he'll have you in bed faster than you can say 'easy lay,' trust me."

I look incredulously at Ruth and we laugh together, a cathartic belly laugh that has us both in tears.

Shutting my office door I relish the tranquillity. I catch up on work pending and soon clear the pile of waiting documents and junk mail. My thoughts then turn to Sebastian as I remember that I haven't replied to his message. I pick up my phone and compose a message to him.

Hi, I'm sorry if I was abrupt and thanks for your offer to help, I appreciate it. I don't think meeting is a good idea though x

As I wait for Sebastian to answer my

message, I fire up my computer and check emails. There's one from Mike and it doesn't make me feel any better.

From: Mike Breeze<mlibreeze1043@hotmail.com>

To: Beth Dove

Sent: Monday 26 November 10:33

Subject: Your Hubby

Beth

Alan's staying with me for a bit. You've really hurt him, which I asked you not to do. It's not good seeing my mate so cut up. Anyway, he wants me to let you know he's seeing a lawyer this pm and suggests you find one too. He's talking about divorce. Get your shit together!

Mike

I feel numb and confused as to why Alan is involving Mike, but understanding that he probably feels that Mike will be able to make me come to my senses. Also we're similar, Alan and I. We both have only a handful of friends, only one whom we can call a best friend in fact, and Mike is Alan's closest friend. I decide not to reply. Let Alan appoint a lawyer, our marriage is doomed. My mood deteriorates further but is lifted by Sebastian's next message.

That's better Elizabeth! Why won't you meet me? What are you afraid of? S

I'm afraid of so many things but most especially I'm afraid of myself, and my lack of self-control. I know very well what will happen if we're alone together.

You! You have a power over me Sebastian and ending up in bed with you is only going to complicate things x

The message is sent. I sit back in my chair and pick up the book I had been reading before all this trouble arose, feeling sure that reading will take my mind off things but am immediately disturbed by my phone's bleep.

That's a great shame Elizabeth as I've gone to the considerable trouble of coming to take you to lunch. I'm parked in The Crescent. See you in 10. S

He's here? Oh my God, is he a bloody stalker? I'm furious … no, that's an understatement - I'm absolutely livid. How dare he *presume*. I've said 'no' to this man and yet he has the audacity to drive three, four hours to… what… take me to lunch?

Snatching my coat and scarf from the hook, I march out of my office without a word to Ruth who watches me leave with a puzzled expression. *Damn him for this. Bloody sodding men!* I seethe.

The rain of late morning is turning to sleet and I pull my scarf up to shield my chin from the biting cold. It's a short walk to The Crescent at the quick pace I maintain. Turning left onto the street, my eyes dart warily in search of his car whilst also watching for Alan in case he's spying on me again – I'm becoming paranoid.

The now familiar Range Rover is parked behind a blue van and as I approach Sebastian becomes visible, talking on his mobile phone. Seeing me step toward his car he reaches across and opens the passenger door for me. I slide onto the warm leather seat - he has thoughtfully switched the seat warmer on in readiness for me. "Yes, yes, Sunday night, fine… yes ready at ten, see you then." He ends his call and turns to face me.

Ready to tear a strip off this arrogant man my arms fold, jaw tense; "what the hell are you doing turning up here, thinking I'll drop everything and have lunch with…" Before I can complete my sentence he kisses me. It is a long hard kiss that I fight for all of five seconds, and then respond to with a hunger and carnal passion that surprises us both.

His right hand strokes my neck and his left hand is travelling up my thigh and I want this man; *need* this man. The more that I tell myself this is wrong, the more I want him. His tongue finds mine and explores my mouth, his teeth catching my lip in his passion. His fingers are pressing into my panties now as he rubs my sex through my thin underwear, all thoughts of admonishing him now gone. His touch feels *so* good. Abruptly he ends the kiss, pulls back his hand and rests back into his seat, his eyes are locked on mine in a serious scowl. "Mmm, delicious thank you," he growls. "So what happened to the Elizabeth who didn't want to see me?" he raises his eyebrow and curls his lip in a mocking smile and I just can't remain angry with this man.

"You're insufferable, De Montfort," I complain.

"I aim to please Mrs. Dove," he smirks. "Put your seat belt on Elizabeth, I'm taking you for that lunch I promised you." I click my seatbelt into place and he pulls out into the traffic and soon we are joining the ring road out of town.

"Where are we going?" I ask, mindful that we mustn't go somewhere Alan may be.

"Wait and see. Patience is a fine attribute, you'd do well to learn some," he says smugly.

We drive for twenty minutes and listen to uplifting music rather than talk, for which I'm grateful and I can feel my tension easing with each mile that passes. Soon Sebastian indicates a right turn and we pull in to a country hotel, which I have not been to before. It looks lovely, much character and very few cars in the car park, certainly not Alan's car nor Mike's.

Sebastian climbs out of the car and opens my door, and I step out. He takes my hand and we walk into the hotel where a log fire burns in the entrance hall. "Wait here," he instructs. He approaches the reception desk and chats to the receptionist for a few minutes, before returning to me clutching a small white card. "Come" he says and again takes my hand. He leads me across the hall to a staircase and it is apparent that we are not dining in the restaurant, but instead heading to a bedroom.

11

I know I should protest – vehemently – and yet I follow him as a lamb to the slaughter, my body tingling in anticipation. At the top stair, Sebastian takes the right turn and we pass through an open fire door, the floorboards creaking as we tread. We stop at the very end door and Sebastian places the modern key card into the lock, which gives, and he opens the door. It momentarily strikes me as odd that such a timeworn hotel should have modern technology.

Stepping into the room, Sebastian pushes

the door shut behind us with his foot and he's upon me immediately, pushing me up against the wall next to the bathroom, his breath quickening. He's kissing and nibbling my neck and while one hand is roughly fondling my left breast, his other is hitching up my skirt.

My arms are around his waist and my hand travels down to his buttocks and I pull him harder against me, wanting him so desperately now. I feel his hand between us and he's unbuttoning his fly, I unbuckle his belt awkwardly, feeling his steely erection through the fabric of his boxer shorts, his smart suit trousers puddle at his feet. He pushes his boxer shorts down and clumsily steps out of his lower clothing. His enormous penis falls heavily into my waiting hand, he sucks in his breath sharply as I squeeze my fingers around his length.

"Fuck, Elizabeth," he groans, nostrils flaring, as I purposefully stroke along his throbbing veins.

I feel his long deft fingers pull roughly at

the tops of my panties. He tugs them down impatiently, and I help him, stepping out of them as they fall to my feet. His hand moves past the tops of my silky hold-up stockings.

"Christ, you're *so* sexy, you're wearing stockings for me, shit that turns me on … I have to have you. Now," he breathes. He lifts me with his hands under my buttocks, wrapping my legs around his waist while I lean back heavily into the wall. The tip of his hard cock finds the entrance to my hot, wet core. He lowers me just enough to allow the slick head of his throbbing member inside me and he teases me with it, allowing it to enter me just an inch before pulling his hips back. Suddenly he drops me hard and the length of his shaft drives into me… so deep that I slap at his back, my fingers biting into his flesh.

As he lifts me again and again, up and down onto his burning shaft, my back slamming into the wall we are oblivious to the world outside the thin wooden hotel door; we are lost in our lust. His cock hits my G-spot and just keeps on thrashing against it and I feel myself building, my mounting climax sending ripples of orgasmic pleasure from my groin until the waves of ecstasy are coursing through me, I cry escapes from deep within my throat. He pulls me down onto him harder, chasing his own climax. He grinds more slowly now, and I feel the sweat on his skin as my fingers splay and pull him even more deeply in to me. He breathes my name into my hair as the convulsions of his release ripple through him, releasing his warm creamy nectar into me.

We slide down into a hot, sticky heap on the floor and lay entwined catching our breath, stroking, kissing and both savouring the moment. When the last embers of our passion have ended, we move to the bed and curl up against the soft pillows. Sebastian closes his eyes and is soon asleep, sated and relaxed. Propping myself up on my arm, I look at him and think how handsome he is with his dark eyebrows, messed up black hair greying at the temples and a shadow of dark stubble on his face. My gaze travels down to his tangle of dark chest hair, which trails down in a thick line past his navel to the bushy mound at his groin. He is so masculine, with an almost primitive ruggedness that I find so sexy. As I study this man intently I am unaware that he has woken and is watching me too.

"You like what you see?" His words make me jump and I blush having been caught staring appreciatively at his body.

"Mm I like, very much!" I purr with a sly grin, and he moves quickly then, flipping me onto my back and straddling me, he pins my arms on either side with his knees and I'm unable to move. He has me trapped. "Sebastian you're a bully let me go!" I protest and laugh simultaneously, but he increases his weight further onto his knees, rendering my attempts to escape entirely futile. "Oh you like to play rough do you?" I ask playfully.

"Oh you have no idea, Mrs. Dove," he replies darkly. "Sure, I like to play rough and I like my women precisely where you are now – restrained and ready for me." He has a cunning grin and an excited gleam in his eyes, he looks so wicked and for a moment I am fearful of what he may have in mind for me next but he kisses my lips and moves off, releasing me. "Another time Elizabeth."

"Sebastian… you're so kinky." It sounds such a puerile statement. He's has roused my curiosity and I want to know more. "I've been looking online and I'm kind of curious about all that Dom/sub stuff."

"And it turns you on," he states knowingly.

"Actually, yes it does. I guess because Alan's totally disinterested in sex and the least dominating man in the world. It's a contrast to my life," I explain. "It's just that I have to be the boss in every element of my life, all my roles are leading roles; at home, at work…I actually find it very appealing to think that a man might take some of that control away from me, tell *me* what to do for once, not put up with my shit," I laugh.

"Where have you been all my life, Elizabeth?" He kisses me again and tenderly strokes my hair. "I'm here for you now darling, you don't have to be in charge any more, in fact I won't *allow* you to be so around me - just so you understand that point. I'd go further to say, if you try and lead me, you'll make me angry Elizabeth." He looks sternly at me and I can sense that he means what he says. This man is used to dominating and asserting his will, and I pity those who try and belittle him – I think he'd make a cruel enemy.

"Have all the women in your life allowed you to dominate them?" I ask.

"They *beg* me to Elizabeth!" He has that sly look again - raised eyebrow, half grin.

"Is that why you like Scarlett working for you, because she's subservient? Does the power that you have over her arouse you?" I'm treading on dangerous ground here, but it seems a good opportunity to push him on this as it bothers me so.

"Don't confuse business with pleasure," he rebukes. "I've got the message, I know you find it bizarre that an attractive woman lives and works at my house but you show me a wealthy, unattached man who wouldn't choose an attractive woman to work for him rather than a hag. I don't intend to justify my choice of employees to you again so the topic is now taboo. Understood?"

"Ok, point taken," I concede. "But you did admit that she was once more to you."

"I felt sorry for her," he says, as though that excuses his actions. "It was a low point in my life and she was there – it was over before it began and she knows her place. She values her job too much to play up."

"Play up? Sebastian, I've seen the way she looks at you ... at us together. Believe me, that woman is in love with you."

"Don't be ridiculous. Change the subject."

"Ok. What was Libby like?" I acquiesce, hoping this next question doesn't also upset him.

"She was the most gentle, beautiful

creature ever to walk the earth. Beautiful but complex, she struggled, you know, with many things in life, not a strong person. Very highly strung she'd get anxious and at the end, paranoid. In the early days when we first met, she was vivacious and spirited. I think not having children was a heavy cross to bear. In the end, she was on all kinds of pills, seeing the best psychologists but she wasn't rational. Her paranoia grew and she began hallucinating. She imagined all manner of things at Penmorrow, accusing me of various wrongdoings and then one day, she just... opted out."

He looks crestfallen, miles away as if he is reliving those last few painful months and days with his mentally sick wife in that old house. Regretting asking him about her I try and lighten his mood. "C'mon, let's have a shower together then I need to get back to work!" I jump off the bed, strip out of my clothes and run stark naked to the bathroom, giggling playfully and hoping he will rise to the bait and come after me. He does not disappoint.

The drive back to my office is more relaxed than our previous journey; my troubles have been temporarily put to the back of my mind. I find myself wishing that Sebastian would take me back to Penmorrow with him. The idea of running away is tempting, if it weren't for the children…

We kiss goodbye in the car, which is parked a hundred yards from my office, and we agree to text each other later tonight. He blows me a kiss as I turn and walk back to work. I'm late for my three o'clock meeting. *What was I thinking?* It's such a crucial meeting; there is so much riding on this.

As I rush into the office, shrugging out of my coat, I see the meeting room is already heaving with people talking and sipping coffee. I dash into the ladies cloakroom to reapply my lipstick and dab a little powder over my still flushed cheeks and smooth down my hair, hoping that I don't reek of sex. Just in case, I spritz myself with perfume from my handbag. *Good to go, they will never guess what I have been up to*, I smirk to myself.

"Hi Beth, you've got a message from Alan to call him back please on his mobile, and Joe's headmaster called – I said you'd call him back after the meeting. There are three contracts to sign on your desk too please, all urgent… oh and Nicky wants to know if she can go ahead and order the new marketing brochures, if so she needs to know today or the deal ends and the price goes up." My secretary is so efficient but the strain builds as my workload and personal issues mount on my shoulders once again.

This meeting is important, since the recession hit in the UK so many firms are struggling to survive. Ours has weathered the storm better than most, however new leads are at an all time low and that is why I had to submit an ambitious tender application for a substantial contract. If we are successful it will mean our projected turnover will double, meaning long awaited growth for Evershaw Dove. Now it seems likely that we will be the preferred bidder, panic has set in as Ruth and

I struggle to raise the considerable financial resources required to meet our contractual obligations.

Staffing is our main concern – we will need to increase our HR team, which of course means advertising, training, and possibly larger offices. We will need to increase our administration support team by two full time members of staff. All of this requires a significant injection of cash; money we don't have.

Alan and I have a colossal mortgage already with a second charge levied on the building by our commercial lender so it's not been possible to leverage any more money against the house. Ruth lives with her mother in her mother's house so, again, that's not a cash source we can utilize. It was therefore an enormous relief when our accountant suggested calling this meeting. He has a network of investors he said, all eager to squirrel away their funds into our sector rather than seeing it exposed to the perils of hedge funds, shares and even high street banks, which are now largely owned by the British public. The syndicate is a long established one, he assured us, with one or two 'new boys' who seem keen to shore up their liquid funds.

If this meeting goes well, we will secure the funds needed to really grow and finally make some decent returns on this business, after years of hard work. Now, more than ever, I am aware of the need for me to be independently solvent if and when Alan and I sell the house, I will be damned before I ask him for money to support me.

Smoothing down my black pencil skirt and straightening the hem of my matching suit jacket, I open the door with a false smile. I schmooze a warm hello, and try to catch the eye of each person in turn, as I begin to shake their hands, and introduce myself. "Elizabeth Dove, how do you do," I gush with my professional voice I have mastered over the years in business. Shaking the next hand extended to meet my firm grip, then the next, "thank you so much for coming today."

As I take the next hand in mine, the touch is familiar but before realisation dawns, it is the dulcet voice which fills my veins with ice. "Sebastian De Montfort, delighted to meet you Elizabeth…" I withdraw my hand sharply and, wide eyed, I stare at him in disbelief and then anger – pure guttural anger at his blatant intrusion into my working life. *What the hell is he doing here?* Why did he not mention that he was invited to attend this meeting when I saw him… only half an hour ago? *Crap.*

12

The room transcends to a sea of faces, all now looking at me expectantly. "Mrs. Dove…?"

I snap back to the moment. "Gentlemen, th…thank you all for coming today." I try to recover my composure and professionalism - this is too important to allow *him* to sabotage my agenda. "In front of you, you will find a presentation pack which includes our business growth plan and forecasts. If I could ask you to please turn to page one, the Executive Summary…" Everyone shuffles the papers in front of them and locates the page as directed. "You will find a synopsis of the structure of our company, a statement on our readiness for market and USP, and a brief outline of our growth plans." The room falls silent as the investors study the document. I lead them through the plan and include a power point presentation, which they digest. When I have finished I open the floor to questions. A portly man of later years and a ruddy complexion raises his hand, "Mrs. Dove…Elizabeth, if we are to invest the monies you require what share interest are you proposing to offer?"

None, I just want your money! "That's a very good question" I reply, "In terms of return on investment we feel that 6% annualized interest plus a 10% share holding is a very generous return, I should add that we would not be offering a Board position, there would be no voting rights attached to the deal."

"Elizabeth…" Sebastian commands my attention. He sits back, arms crossed and a wicked glint in his eyes – he is relishing my discomfort. I stare at him with the coldest, steely glare I can muster. "With all due respect, you cannot expect investors to simply write a cheque for the level of funding you are seeking, and expect them to be happy with a return they would achieve from a high street bank with little or no risk exposure. I personally would require a non executive Board position, in addition to 20% of your ordinary shareholding."

Oh I just bet you would, you control freak.

I am furious with Sebastian for demeaning me in front of these men, and for sowing the seed in their fat little heads about wanting a slice of our company. Well, it's not up for negotiation – *over my dead body*! This business has pretty much cost me my marriage, my social life, years of stress… if he thinks I am going to hand it on a plate then he is crazier than I gave him credit for. "Thank you *Mister* De Montfort" I say with more than a hint of bitterness. "As I just indicated, the option of a Board position is not something we would consider at this time."

Averting my frosty gaze from him, my attention returns to the others in the room. "Please remember gentlemen, that you would be receiving a very healthy *profit* share as well as an attractive interest rate on your investment – that is not something you would receive from your high street bank," that told *him*. He looks impassive but raises an eyebrow at me, shakes his head and writes something down.

I answer questions from two gentlemen and thankfully these are operational rather than financial queries. Drained, I sit down again as Ruth stands to deliver a closing speech. Looking at the faces of the men, I can't read their expressions in order to guess whether or not they may bite the cherry.

Avoiding Sebastian's gaze, instead I look everywhere except at him; I'm simply too angry with him but I feel his eyes burning into me and it takes all my willpower to avert my eyes. Ruth is thanking everyone for attending the meeting today, and for their interest in Evershaw Dove. Soon I'm shaking hands with them all as they leave, most muttering that they will 'be in touch' and 'very interesting proposal' but no firm offers.

Sebastian is waiting behind the last gentleman, who is telling me he will give the matter his 'earnest consideration' and I turn to follow him through the door but I feel a firm grip on my arm forcing me back into the meeting room. Ruth has left the room and I see that she's in deep conversation with our accountant so I am alone with *him*. He shuts the door and leans against it, arms folded and an amused smirk plastered across his face. I let him have it.

"You arrogant, conceited, son-of-a-bitch!" I hiss. "What the *hell* do you think you are doing coming here like this, no bloody warning, making me look an idiot... it's all a game to you isn't it?"

I am on a roll and the venom spills forth.

"Oh it's just fine to turn up here out of the blue, take me to a hotel and have your way with me, no mention of the *real* reason you are here which is to bleed my company dry. Oh no, the sex was a nice little added bonus wasn't it... a little extra for your trouble in driving up here...I... I'm lost for words."

"Have you finished your little rant Elizabeth?" The patronising twerp asks. I cannot speak to him. I cannot find any more words to relay how angry I am. "Because if you have, then please allow me to respond. Sit down."

Staring aghast at him, I cannot believe that he dares to order me to sit so I remain standing with my defensive posture of folded arms, chin in the air.

"SIT." He barks, pulling a chair away from the table and swishing his hand toward it indicating that I should sit. I sit, cross my legs and arms and look straight ahead out of the window rather than in his direction, like a petulant child once more, sitting before her head teacher for a reprimand. "That's better. I appreciate that it was a shock to see me here, but the fact is that I knew very well that you would not have allowed me to come had

I discussed it with you first. Yes, I did want to see you other than in the boardroom... although I have to admit that I would rather like to fuck you *hard* over this table right now... but that aside, I thought we would kill two birds with one stone, so to speak. I had you to myself before the meeting, let's call it 'due diligence' Elizabeth. Plus, I was then privy to a very interesting business meeting at which a sexy, clever woman convinced me to part with a large chunk of my money and not many people achieve that so very well done you."

My jaw has dropped and I am totally and utterly speechless. He doesn't see that this is wrong on so many levels. He wants to *fuck* me over the table - hard! He is going to lend me the money... *oh and he wants to fuck me over the boardroom table*. My mind keeps on returning to that point and I'm so furious with him. "Fine" I say petulantly, "10% and I'll shake on the deal here and now." I have him now, the cocky little prick will never agree to a reduction in terms so he will walk away and I shall have won and proven that he cannot always get what he wants.

"10% it is" he rises and proffers a hand to shake.

What the hell? We shake hands, his grip so tight on mine that I wince. "I'd have gone to 15%" I tell him smugly after the deal is sealed with a shake, his hand still gripping mine.

"And I, Elizabeth, would have dropped to 5%." *Damn him.*

He doesn't release my hand, his grip like iron. He's close to me, and I feel his breath on my neck as he pulls me forward and kisses my cheek. He's clever, anyone looking through the sound proofed glass would see us shaking on a deal and him politely kissing the cheek of a newly acquired business partner, nothing more sinister. Yet he's hurting me now, not releasing me and I start to protest and pull at my hand but he maintains his hold on me. "Come to Cornwall this weekend, Elizabeth. Drive down to Penmorrow and be with me."

"You really are *nuts*" I hiss at him, incredulously. "You may be investing in our company but don't for a minute underestimate me and think that you are buying *me*. I won't be driving anywhere this weekend. I will be here trying to sort the tatters of my marriage and… if I never see you again it will be too soon."

He releases my sore hand and I turn, open the door and flee to the ladies cloakroom where I lock myself in a cubicle, and sob with the humiliation and stress of the day.

Ruth is tapping lightly on the door and asking me what's wrong. I open the door and fall into her arms and she hugs me tightly. "Beth you did really well don't cry" she soothes.

"You don't understand," I wail. "He's agreed to give us the money for 5% *damn him*."

"What? That's fantastic news, why on earth are you crying? Which one was it? I bet it was that gorgeous black haired Adonis, he couldn't take his eyes off you…" she says excitedly.

"Yes, but don't you see … that was Sebastian! It's all about control, he wants to *own* me Ruth and now I've agreed to his investment I've walked straight into his plan and…sold my soul to the *devil!*" I sob.

"Let me deal with him, Beth. To be honest I would rather enjoy 'dealing' with him, he's so sexy!"

I flash her an angry glare at which she blushes.

"Look, we take his money, grow the business, and we need never see him again. He'll receive his money via our accountant and, meanwhile, you get on with your life. Get yourself sorted, divorce Alan, think about yourself and the kids and don't complicate it further with Mr Moneybags." She says wisely.

"You don't know what he's like" I protest. "He won't let it go Ruth, he'll be all over our business like a rash – he's a control freak."

"I'll deal with him Beth, leave the creep to me. The main thing is we've got our money, we can go ahead with our plans."

"Be careful," I warn, "I'm discovering just how manipulative he can be."

13

Alan's mobile phone rings as I return his earlier call. He picks up and I can hear the acrimony in his tone.

"Beth. Thanks for *eventually* getting back to me. I've spoken to my lawyer and it seems that, if we can agree things amicably, we can get the divorce through without having to incur huge legal bills each and, to be honest, I'd rather we sorted everything as soon as possible."

He tells me I can have the house but he

wants his pension and his share of the business if and when it is sold. He then talks about custody of the children, clearly having written all his terms down before my call, stating the children must stay with him on alternate weekends and two nights during the week plus half of their school holidays.

"Another thing" he says, *there's more?* "You are NOT to have a man back to MY house at any time... understand?"

I do not counter his vexatious request with the fact that it's also *my* house. Instead, I agree to his terms, which overall seem reasonable. He ends the call by informing me that his lawyer will prepare a draft agreement and then send me the divorce papers and then he clicks off. I'm left feeling partly relieved that we have reached an agreement on which to move forward, but also a profound sadness at the ending of our marriage.

I return the call to Joe's school and ask to speak to the head teacher who advises me that

Joe will be excluded from lessons tomorrow morning for telling Mrs. Elmore, his history teacher, to "fuck off" – *can today get any worse?*

He will be required to sit in the school library and write a letter of apology to Mrs. Elmore, who apparently has never been spoken to in such a manner before; I somehow doubt that as I recall her as being an irritating, mousy, woman with a squeaky voice and cynical attitude to her pupils. I apologise profusely, and explain that Joe is going through a difficult time at home as his father has now left the family home - this news is not met with empathy by the Catholic head teacher of Joe's Catholic school. I'm not surprised, but the school needs to know that my Joe has his reasons for being rebellious right now.

Ending the call, I hurriedly sign the waiting contracts on my desk and call Nicky to authorise the ordering of new brochures, figuring we can afford them now we have the investment. That returns my thoughts to Sebastian and his meddling. *What am I to do with that man?* I wonder. Never before have I been so… so subjugated by any man, and I detest the part of me, which welcomes his dominance. It's as though I'm two people – Elizabeth Dove the respectable mother and business woman… and some harlot who dwells in my darkest psyche; she wears red lace underwear, a black choker and bends over saying "whip me now baby!" and I can't recall her always being there, perhaps she's been asleep and Sebastian has awoken her?

My phone bleeps.

Hi PARTNER. I hope you keep that boardroom table polished Mrs. Dove I intend to have you there – perhaps after our next board meeting? S

He's so obtuse. *Partner!* He may have wiled his way onto the Board but he will not be receiving any extra 'benefits' from me any more. My reply is curt and I hope it stings.

Mr. De Montfort, Ruth will be your point of contact here, I don't deal with minority shareholders. B

He is quick to reply.

Interesting. Hope Ruth has great legs too and likes tables. S

Insufferable ass. I can't resist a cutting reply.

I'll be sure to give her the choker! B

I wait for his reply but my phone stays silent. I'm full of regret then. For some reason he's under my skin and, although I try to despise him, I find myself wanting him even more.

I begin to wonder if this is just escapism; if my life has been so lacking in male attention that I am pouncing upon the first male who shows me attention. Perhaps he strokes my female ego, I begin to tell myself that I'd be better served gleaning satisfaction from books and my vibrating toys rather than suffer the complexities and manipulations of men.

Time to call it a day, it's five thirty and the kids will be home waiting for dinner having taken the bus home from school. I hate them having to take the bus but I had no choice again today.

When I arrive home the house seems strangely empty without Alan. Joe's engrossed in with his games console, blowing apart a zombie while Bella pretends to complete homework; she thinks I haven't noticed the instant messages on the screen of her PC.

There is precious little food in the fridge so I retrieve a ready made chicken curry from the freezer, *defrost thoroughly before use*, the packaging advises. I remove the cardboard surround and stab the plastic film lid aggressively with a fork then toss the whole solid, frozen mass into the oven onto a baking tray and turn the dial to the highest temperature. It's an improvement on most of my culinary attempts – most food items are prepared using my 'ten minute microwave rule' and miraculously I haven't poisoned us yet!

The children and I sit at the kitchen table and eat our insipid curry, and I realise I miss the family dinners we used to enjoy around the dining table with everyone talking in turn about their day. The normal activities of living seem so far removed suddenly, and I feel a stabbing of remorse and sadness in the pit of my stomach. *No good dwelling on the past, I've got to move on* I tell myself.

Joe's in bed asleep, Bella's gone back to her bedroom and I'm alone and feeling miserable. I pour myself a large glass of red wine in the kitchen and take it to the lounge where I sink down onto the sofa, exhausted.

My iPad is on the coffee table and I pick it up and rest it on my lap, reaching forward and picking up my glass. I wake my tablet and, as the screen comes to life, I take a long drink of wine and savour the warm richness and allow my thoughts to drift to Sebastian. I can still feel his touch on my skin and see the wicked glint in his eyes when he looks at me.

It's nearly nine o'clock and not too late to send him a message so I pick up my phone from the coffee table, replacing it with my wine, and send a text message.

Hey, you busy?

Staring at my phone, I wait for his reply. A few minutes later my phone alerts me to a new message received but it is not from Sebastian. It's from Alan and he's obviously drunk.

Hope ur happy Beth ruin our marriage for wot? Never good nuff for you well I want the kids I'm a better bloody parent than you

His message fills me with dread and anger; a can feel a knot in my stomach tighten and, made braver by the wine, tap a hasty reply.

Piss off Alan! You're hardly blameless in our marriage breaking up are you?! As for the kids I hardly think a court in the land would give custody to a whisky soaked drunk!

Shaking, I send the message and drain my glass. *If it's a fight he wants, he can bloody have one!*

My phone bleeps in my lap, I hesitantly look at the screen.

Hey sexy, lovely to hear from you – still angry with me? S

I'm angry with all men, honey, not just you!

Deciding I've had enough of men for today, I switch my phone off and go to bed without replying.

The next morning Joe is brooding and quiet when I drive him to school, Bella has insisted on taking the bus again and I'm unsure as to whether she is angry and blaming me for her father leaving or just showing the first signs of maturity and independence. Chatting to Joe in the car, my light conversation is met with grunts and one-word answers and he is keen to get out when we reach school.

At the office I have a heap of paperwork waiting for my attention, which I plough through by late morning. Ruth is at a meeting with our lawyer to discuss Sebastian's investment and shareholding.

My work completed, I wonder whether to bunk off for the rest of the day. Instead I decide upon a little much needed 'me' time and welcome distraction. Taking my latest raunchy book from the drawer in my desk, I flick through the chapters until I reach a particularly erotic scene. They are ensconced in a secret room, her hands and ankles are bound with rope and he is applying clamps to her nipples. *Ouch*, it makes me shudder and suddenly I'm more curious than ever about this perverse form of sex.

I fire up my computer, and tilt the screen to an angle so that no one entering my office will witness my search. There are numerous online pages offering a plethora of deviancy, ranging from torturous equipment, to bondage and sadism/masochism dating websites. A forum for submissive women catches my attention and reading the threads, I recognise many of my needs and desires within those postings. The women talk about dominant men who care for them and ensure they are safe and looked after, yet with the expectation and profound understanding that their submissive meets their every desire enthusiastically and tirelessly and without question or disobedience. The primary attraction for me, apart from the hot sex, is that the woman is not expected or required to be the decision maker or alpha of the relationship.

Reflecting on my own marriage and my career, I can see that this is parallel to my own life and realize that I've been craving a significant life change for some years. Perhaps submission is the panacea to my unhappiness and dissatisfaction with my life. The penny drops, this is why I'm attracted to Sebastian – he holds the key to unlocking and freeing 'me'. *Go with it Beth, life is short and it's your turn to fly.*

Picking up the phone, I tap Sebastian's number. My hand is trembling slightly and the knot in my stomach is firmly twisting … *feel the fear and do it anyway…*

Sebastian answers and his deep sexy voice turns the knot in my stomach to a warm tingling in my groin. He reassures me with his confident tone, listening to me as I dump all my anguish and feelings on his shoulders. He tells me exactly what I so need to hear. My marriage breakdown was not my fault as it had clearly been on the cards for years, and it is now *my* time to do fulfil my own desires. It's nearly Christmas he reminds me, the children will find this year tough because we won't be a family unit. We must come to stay at Penmorrow for the holiday season. He doesn't allow me to interject as, he assures me, he knows best and I must trust him on this.

My mobile phone rings – number withheld, I accept the call.

"Elizabeth Dove speaking."

"Sorry ... I must have the wrong number." The voice sounds familiar.

"Who are you trying to reach?" I ask.

"Rosie. I don't know her surname." It's

Simon!

"Erm … hold the line, I'll get her for you." I place the phone down in my lap for a full minute, before picking it up again. Changing my voice to a slightly higher octave, I say, "Rosie speaking."

"Rosie, hi. It's Simon."

"Simon, what a lovely surprise. How are you?"

"I'm good. How are you?" *Awkward conversation!*

"I'm fine thanks. How's work?" *Think of something to say, Beth.*

"Work's good. Not many fires though." *Blimey he's boring.*

"Well, that's a good thing right?" I say lightly.

"Guess so."

"So, Simon. What can I do for you?" *Say something for God's sake before one of us dies …*

"Just thought I'd phone for a chat. See how you are." *So, get chatting!*

"How lovely. I enjoyed our time together," I lie.

"Yeh, me too," he says.

"Well then …"

"Wanna do it again?" asks Simon. *And they say the art of romance is gone.*

"You bet." Another lie. "Let's fix something up really soon. I'm busy for the next couple of weeks but why don't you text me some dates and we'll put something in the diary." *Like maybe next century.*

"Yeh. Sounds like a plan. See ya." He cuts the call before 'Rosie' can say goodbye.

At the end of the day, my desk is tidy and I turn out the office lights and put my coat on. My phone pings with a new text message.

Rosie I can do next Wednesday or the

following Monday. Any good? Same hotel, same hot sex. Simon x

Oh crap! I tap a quick reply to him.

Hi Simon, sorry can't make either of those days due to meetings. Will call you. X

Don't hold your breath!

Driving home I scold myself for getting into these tricky situations. There's no comparison between Sebastian and Simon. Sebastian is complicated – *very* complicated but at least he doesn't have a vacuous void for a brain. I make a mental note to delete the message from Simon – erase him from my life but that thought is forgotten, as my mind drifts back to thoughts of Sebastian.

14

The weeks pass so quickly. Each day is a master class of juggling; the children, housework, the business, divorce correspondence and I am utterly and completely exhausted, both mentally and physically.

My mother tries to help as much as she can and is invaluable, as is Ruth and between the three of us we somehow manage always to keep the cogs and wheels of my life well oiled and turning. The children have not yet starved or burned the house down on the days I have worked late, thanks to mother being there. The business has not suffered from my drop in efficiency thanks to Ruth shouldering more than her share of meetings - life after Alan is bearable.

Alan is not thriving alone. He doesn't appear to be at work very much and the children tell me, after their latest visit with him that he's on 'garden leave' meaning suspension; for what misconduct I have no idea, although I suspect whisky may be involved. Bella tells me he's drinking all the time – when I question her on this she clams up, loyal to her father but it spurs me to notify my lawyer, seeking a reduction in his access and restricting him from driving our children in case he is under the influence of alcohol. His fury at the ensuing letter culminates in the mother of all rows on the phone late one night, when he accuses me of being a manipulating bitch who is 'just like all those women and no wonder Justice For Fathers were in the news every day when women like me stopped them seeing their kids'. There is no reasoning with him and it leaves me with a steely resolve to continue the restriction, as the safety and welfare of my children seems to be my priority alone, not Alan's.

This new confidence is directly attributable to Sebastian. Our daily telephone conversations reaffirm my decisions and actions, and Sebastian's wise words and practical suggestions prove invaluable in helping survive each day rather than curling up in my bed and closing out the world as I wanted to do soon after Alan left me.

Christmas is fast approaching. The children have just two more days before their schools close for the holidays, and I have just two more days to work until the start of my two week period of leave and I can hardly wait. The anticipation of seeing Sebastian again after so many weeks, together with the promise of a much needed rest are steering me through each day. Alan vehemently refuses to allow the children to spend the entire holiday with me and I relent – agreeing that he can have them to stay with him for New Year. I decide he is less likely to drink himself into oblivion on New Year's Eve if the children are with him. It also means they can travel to Penmorrow with me for Christmas, we leave in just four days time.

Mother is unhappy that the children and I will be absent for Christmas, but she has decided to invite her sister, Aunty Margaret, to travel from Eastbourne and enjoy the festivities with her. They are not close but my mother will nevertheless enjoy her company and it absolves me from my selfish act of going away. My penance for such a sin was to agree to host dinner for the two of them on the night before we leave for Cornwall and we exchange gifts over an early turkey dinner at my home before kissing and hugging our farewells and festive wishes.

The white carpet of frost glistens on the front lawn and path, twinkling in the early morning sun as I load suitcases and brightly wrapped Christmas presents into the boot of my car. The children seem in good spirits, chatting animatedly for much of the journey.

They seem unconcerned to be visiting a stranger or spending Christmas with him, instead they seem more anxious to know whether I have bought Joe's latest console game, and Bella's iPad, as demanded on their hastily penned Christmas wish lists, which of course I have. "Kids, are you excited to be staying in a mansion for Christmas?" I ask, observing the reaction on their faces in my rear view mirror.

"Bella told me it's haunted," replies Joe nervously, "and she said there will be dungeons and secret tunnels and everything," he muses. Bella laughs, "*belieeever!*" and Joe digs her ribs sharply with his elbow. Bella yelps and responds with a hefty thump to Joe's leg giving him a dead leg. I sigh, this is my life these days but I resist the urge to scream at my children or to dampen my excitement, instead I switch on the radio and crank the volume up to drown out their squabbles.

We break our journey only for a comfort

stop near Exeter and to share out the hastily made sandwiches, which are in the picnic bag beside me. Fifty minutes later I leave the arterial road to north Cornwall and am soon navigating the tiny capillary lanes threading toward Trevissey. It's odd but the smaller the roads, the greater my excitement as we approach the turning to Penmorrow. We soon pass the stone stags, and the children gasp as the grandeur of Penmorrow looms ahead.

15

The car wheels crunch noisily on the gravel signalling our arrival. As I cut the ignition I see, reflected in the wing mirror, the welcome sight of Sebastian approaching from the house.

The children are already out of the car and, as I open my door and step from the car, the sight of Sebastian embracing Bella and shaking Joe's hand melts my heart. I'm beaming when he walks over to me. He puts his arms around my waist and pulls me tightly into his chest, kissing my forehead. My arms wrap around him and I turn my head upwards

and plant a lingering, intense kiss on his lips –
I'm so very glad to be with him again, having
grown to miss him terribly over the last few
weeks.

After an eternity of kissing we become
aware of the children, impatient to get on with
the business of ghost hunting and exploring
the vast house before them. Sebastian opens
the car boot and retrieves our luggage, which
he carries into the house. The children run
ahead of him and, as I follow him inside, a
feeling of optimism and belonging enfolds
me. *I am home.*

Two hours. The time it takes the children
to complete their mission of discovery, after
which they find us in the kitchen and regale us
with tales of dark shadows and 'really cool'
rooms. Sebastian feigns intrigue, then fuels
their excitement by telling them stories of an
apparition of a grey lady purportedly seen
floating along the upper landing and passing
through bedroom doors. I laugh and
admonish him for telling tales, which will

inevitably keep Joe awake tonight.

Sebastian leaves us at three, returning an hour later with the most enormous Christmas tree the children have ever seen. We have a wonderful time adorning the branches with the glass baubles that Sebastian retrieves from the attic.

It feels cathartic – to laugh, to be a family unit, to forget Alan and all the negativity which has clouded my life of late. It's Christmas and I feel safe, my children are happy – life is good once again.

Scarlett serves a delicious supper of beef wellington with a warm chocolate fondant for dessert and, irritatingly, joins us at the table.

"Beats your microwave dinners, Mum!" exclaims my ungrateful son as he devours his second helping. Scarlett catches my eye and I note the smugness with which she smiles at me.

In the great hall, the last embers of the fire glow and the last remnant of burning pine spits cinders and crackles. Refreshed from a hot bath and now dressed only in a towelling robe, I'm sitting on the rug with Sebastian, as we did the night we met, gazing at the fire and sipping port. We don't speak but instead relish each other's closeness. The house is quiet. The children are sleeping upstairs and the only sounds I can hear come from the fire and the grandfather clock in the entrance hall chiming intermittently. I'm seated between Sebastian's open legs, resting back against his strong chest. I raise the crystal port glass to my lips, finishing the warm sweet liquid and breathe in the aroma of smoky pine, sighing contentedly. He kisses the back of my neck then nibbles at the top of my ear and I moan at the touch of his lips, "mm that feels so good…"

"We aim to please, Elizabeth… and how does this feel?" he moves the hair from my neck and traces gentle kisses down to the top of my spine, sending small tremors down my spine to my sacrum. I squirm and melt back against him harder. It feels so good. He falls back with my weight against him, onto the rug taking me with him – my glass tumbling from my grasp. His legs entwine mine, and we're kissing passionately, our tongues seeking each other's with a raw hunger. His hands roughly grasp and knead my breasts, pinching my nipples until I cry out with the delicious pain. He moves on top of me, my legs now wrapped tightly around his, pulling his hardness against me and I need him so badly, the ache within me is almost unbearable.

My hand moves down to his hardness, stroking the length of him through the course fabric of his jeans and he groans, reaching down to unzip his fly – his manhood rises, freed from the constraints of the denim. He hurriedly pulls at the tie belt of my robe until it gives, the robe falling open to expose my nakedness. His hand moves between my legs, his fingers probing my creamy arousal, his thumb stroking at my clitoris so expertly. He continues his assault on my clit as I stroke his throbbing member, my teeth catching his lip as the passion of our kiss engulfs us. He sits up then, pulling me with him and positioning me to straddle him.

My legs still wrapped around him, I feel the slick head of his cock pressing at my wetness as he grabs my hips and purposefully guides me down onto his shaft. He is pounding into me again and again as his grip on my hips controls the pace of our movements, forcing me to ride him faster and faster, down harder and deeper - chasing our orgasms together. I feel the delicious waves coursing through me as I grind down harder, taking all of him greedily. His breath catches as he finds his own his release, the spasms of his climax shuddering through my core. The strength leaves my body as my climax abates - I sag forward into his arms, not daring to move my hips or legs, wanting him inside me still. Savouring this moment neither of us moves, and the dying fire throws just enough heat to warm my buttocks and back.

"You're so amazing…" I whisper. "This is what I've been missing all these years." At this moment I feel a flood of warm emotion and gratitude toward Sebastian. *Could this be love?*

"You're pretty amazing too, Mrs. Dove," he murmurs as he plants a gentle kiss on my forehead. He strokes my hair as he holds me. I've longed for this for so long, fantasising and imagining how good sex could be. I feel almost drunk with contentment right now. Our breathing steadies, my eyes are heavy and I listen to the faint ticking of the Grandfather clock mirroring Sebastian's heartbeat and breathing and it lulls me. My eyes lazily adjust to the growing darkness of the room as the fire fizzles out... *and then I see her!*

16

A shadow at first, it could be the failing light playing tricks on my eyes but then the shadow moves … the shape is that of a woman, I'm certain. It moves from its position by the long heavy drapes at the mullioned window and glides silently toward the door. My breath catches.

I sit up and my eyes are wide now, trying desperately to focus and the doorway is more illuminated with the light from the hallway casting sufficient yellow glow upon the shadow to reveal that it is not a ghost, it's *her...* Scarlett. "Oh my God," I gasp, "Scarlett was right here ... *watching us!*"

I feel his body stiffen. "Where?" he asks and I detect just a hint of annoyance in his voice, but certainly not the shock that I feel and that unnerves me.

"Over by the window, she must have been watching us the whole time. When I saw her she left."

"Don't be ridiculous, Elizabeth," he scoffs. "Why the hell would Scarlett be watching us? Anyway, so what if she was?" *So what?* Is this another, freaky 'normality' in this house? Voyeurism certainly is not normal in my humble opinion and after ... what we did! I'm furious suddenly, and I want answers from her, as it's painfully obvious that none shall be forthcoming from him.

"I'm sorry Sebastian, it may be perfectly acceptable to you but not to me. I'm going to ask her what the hell she was doing spying on us." I get up quickly pulling my robe tightly around me, tie the belt firmly, and leave before he has the opportunity to stop me. I exit the great hall and make my way to the kitchen but when I enter, the room is empty.

Instinct takes me to Sebastian's study next and I find the door ajar. I can hear Sebastian moving around in the great hall, and imagine that he's hastily putting on his clothes and is sure to follow me. I move hastily through the doorway, which hides the steps to the basement and, flicking the light switch on, begin my descent.

Scarlett's door is closed but I don't bother knocking. I firmly twist the handle and open the door, to find Scarlett sat at her dressing table brushing her long dark hair. She turns as I enter her room, her rosebud lips pursed at the intrusion. "Excuse me, don't you ever knock?" she asks indignantly.

"No I don't bloody well knock, and I hardly think *you* should be questioning me so bloody huffily, when you just spied on us having sex!" I reply, rage turning my cheeks red now, my hands firmly on my hips in a challenging stance.

"Believe me, *Elizabeth,* you've a lot to learn if you find that so disconcerting," she retorts and continues languidly brushing her glossy locks.

"What the hell's that supposed to mean?" I screech. She' still brushing, and I'm tempted to rip out a handful of her lustrous dark hair at this point.

"What exactly upset you? Was it the fact that you were watched - or the fact that you were watched doing things you haven't done before?"

I'm horrified by her insolence but she continues. "Because it seems to me, Elizabeth, that you're ashamed and truly, you have nothing to be ashamed about – it's all perfectly natural." I take a step back, trying to comprehend what she's saying to me.

"It's *not* natural Scarlett … to watch two people having sex is absolutely not natural, and I don't think Sebastian is happy at all about you watching us."

"Oh? I think you'll find he's fine about it Elizabeth, why don't you ask him?" The blatantly disrespectful harlot has gone too far, and I intend to see to it that Sebastian dismisses her ass immediately.

"Ask me what?" Sebastian stands in the doorway, one arm resting on the frame and the other stroking his chin, his expression unreadable. I spin around and beseech him to take action against the tramp.

"She admits spying on us Sebastian! You have to fire her ..." I exclaim in exasperation, ignoring his question. His eyes are on hers I notice, not mine and I click my fingers at him impatiently to snap his attention back to me.

"Admits it hmm?" he turns his gaze to me now. "Some people find it rather erotic being watched. Does that not turn you on?" he asks, his eyebrow arched awaiting my reply. I'm speechless.

"*Hello?* Am I the only person here who has a sense of decency?" my high-pitched voice enquires, my eyes darting from him to her. Neither of them shows any sign of remorse. Each has a smile on their lips – a *knowing* smile as if they're part of a club and I'm the outsider, not party to some secret handshake or coded language.

Scarlett sighs, puts her hairbrush down onto her dressing table and rises. She's wearing a sheer white night dress made of delicate tulle, the thin straps barely supporting the floaty garment. I can see the dark shadow of her nipples through the fabric - the outline of her slim figure silhouetted by the lamp on her nightstand. She's so beautiful – an ethereal beauty. I feel sure Sebastian has noticed her near nudity.

"Come Elizabeth," he proffers his hand toward me but I ignore it, shooting him a disdainful glare. I want him to object and hiss at her but instead he continues to hold out his hand to me. He's staring at Scarlett - at that moment I'm sure that they are still lovers, and it sickens me to my core. Scarlett steps toward me and she, too, reaches out for me.

I'm between them both. Each is reaching for me and yet I trust neither and I back away from both, until I feel the cold metal of her bed frame behind my knees.

She reaches me, where I stand, her arms encircling me. She embraces my rigid body – rendered immobile by the shock of her audacity - her lips close to my ears, her warm breath against my neck and she whispers, "everything's fine, sweet girl, you have nothing to worry about, you're here where you belong ..." She releases me from her embrace and pads barefoot to Sebastian's side where they both regard me with matching smirks. "I think we'll be good friends Elizabeth, we've a lot in common – more than you think," she says.

"Ok, I get it," I snarl. "It's still going on isn't it?" I look from one to the other but neither seems to be willing to explain anything to me. Then Sebastian moves toward me and takes my hand, pulling me down with him to sit on the side of the bed. He looks up at Scarlett and I notice the coldness in her expression as she eyes Sebastian's arm around my waist protectively, she averts her eyes from his.

"I'd rather eat my own eyeballs, than be friends with you, lady," I hiss at Scarlett.

Scarlett sighs resignedly. "You need to lighten up. You really do not want to make an enemy of me, trust me."

"Is that a threat?" I yell, harnessing the last remnants of self-control so as not to slap her smug face.

"Enough, you two," he barks sharply. Leave us Scarlett, I want to talk to Elizabeth in private."

"Yes Sir, if you need me I'll be in the kitchen, I'll make cocoa." She closes the bedroom door behind her and we're alone.

I chew my lip nervously, feeling unexpectedly self-conscious in his presence now and feeling angry and hurt too. Jealous – I feel insanely jealous of the bond that the two of them clearly share. "I want to know," I declare. "If you and Scarlett still sleep together then I have a right to know, though how you manage to maintain the charade of 'employer,' I have no idea. It's just plain weird Sebastian - plain weird and wrong." He's still clutching my hand in his and when I try to withdraw it he increases his grip.

"We don't sleep together Elizabeth, I promise you that," he says quietly.

"I don't believe you," I whisper, tears pricking my eyes as my dreams are shattered, as the brutal reality of his betrayal crushes my heart. Then the anger boils within me. "No, I get it. God I'm stupid; you have free sex with me – hell it's probably a novelty for you not to have to pay for it! Shit, I'm so stupid, men are all the same; why did I think you'd be different?"

He places a finger across my lips to hush me and turns my chin so that he's looking into my watery eyes. "It's not like that Elizabeth, and you'll see that if you give me … us … a chance. This isn't about me - it's about *you*. You've been goodness knows how many years living a frigid and suppressed existence and what you'll find here is the panacea to your discontent. You've so many insecurities. Fuck, what has he done to you? You see only the darkness, never the light."

He wipes away the tears, which roll down my cheek, but I flinch at his touch, confused at his aptitude for turning the tables so intuitively, when I am still mad at him.

"I want to unlock your deepest desires and release your inhibitions and frustration my darling. Think of your time here with me as your time to be who you want to be. No one here will judge you or disapprove of anything you do or say. Equally, you must afford the same courtesy to me, to live as I please and be who I am, without judging me or thinking you can change me. You *have* to trust me. Everything I do, or ask you to do, is in your best interests. Do you trust me?"

"I don't know… I want to but it's all so far removed from my normal life. To lose control, like you want me to, is so alien to me. I need time. Shit, I feel jealous of *her*. You have to understand that I've no self-confidence any more. I doubt myself all the time. Why the hell are you with me?"

He pauses while he digests what I've said to him. "You're my girlfriend Elizabeth, my *love*. I'll take care of you and the children, and I'll allow you to experience things that you've never even fantasised about. You can pass your fears, your insecurities to me to shoulder them for you, and the *real* Elizabeth can be free and unburdened. Now, isn't that tempting?" It is tempting, so enticing but so wrong. He seems to know exactly how to tap into my psyche, to extract my weaknesses and vulnerabilities and lay them bare in front of me. I find myself aroused by his offer – like Eve wanting to take a bite of the forbidden fruit, aware of the dire consequences, but giving in to temptation regardless.

I've always been one to push boundaries and take risks, never overly dwelling on the consequences of my actions, nor analysing potential pitfalls prior to choosing a path to follow. It doesn't surprise me how easily I push aside the weird freakery of this house. My inner she-devil is awakening after a seventeen-year hibernation, and I'm sure there is little that can stop her.

"I don't want to be made to feel jealous about Scarlett. What you do when I'm not here is up to you but when I am here, you are only with me. Understood?" *What on earth am I suggesting? It will never be alright for him to be with her, under any circumstances.*

"Only you," he sooths. "There *is* only you, anything Scarlett and I shared was superficial and short-lived. I've told you this before. She's a vulnerable girl and sometimes her expectations and romanticism needs to be tempered, and I will do so. She's not a threat to us, Elizabeth."

"She needs to be reminded to respect our privacy. You and she may think it's ok to do all manner of things, but I'm not like that."

His hand strokes my back in comforting circular movements. His deep hazel eyes are unflinching as they stare into my soul. "We just live a more liberal lifestyle here. Don't judge us. Just know how I feel about *you*."

"It's bloody perverse though," I counter. He shakes his head in apparent exasperation before leading me from Scarlett's bedroom.

There is so very much to absorb and think about, but right now, I am exhausted. I'll think about all this evening's weirdness in the morning. It's Christmas Eve and I want my children to have a happy day tomorrow.

17

Christmas morning has dawned. It's a magical vista from the house this morning - it's a bright crisp day, a heavy overnight frost glistens across the expansive grounds, a scattering of deer stand majestically, like reindeer, across the paddocks.

I wake a sleepy Bella at nine, by which time Joe is excited enough to combust. Scarlett is already busily peeling vegetables, by the time we all gather in the kitchen. She and I work together, preparing breakfast of smoked salmon and deliciously creamy scrambled eggs. Neither of us mentions our altercation, and she is particularly friendly toward me it seems. Certain that her motives are disingenuous I remain cautious, but refuse to allow her to dampen my high spirits. We all breakfast together, seated around the kitchen table, the children guessing what their gifts may be. I feel more excited than the children. Even when they were tiny, I would be the first to wake - banging noisily about the house to wake the children so that we could open our presents. Alan was never one for Christmas preferring to slope off to the pub for a late morning whisky than to share in the festivities.

The Christmas tree which Sebastian bought yesterday gives off a wonderfully fragrant pine scent and the tiny coloured lights twinkle on its' branches. At the base of the tree, which sits next to the fireplace in the great hall, is a small mountain of brightly wrapped gifts. I have placed my gifts to Sebastian and the children at the back of the pile, so that the children don't snoop.

Scarlett has already put the enormous

free-range turkey into the range to slowly roast and the aroma from the kitchen is divine.

Mother calls after breakfast and the children and I chat excitedly to her, and end the call wishing her and my aunt a very merry Christmas. I tell her I miss her dreadfully but that we are all having a wonderful time. I make a mental note to spoil her next year to make up for being absent this holiday season.

Next I call Ruth, who is bursting with questions as to how Sebastian and I are getting along. It's difficult to talk openly as the children are beside me but I tell her everything is wonderful and we exchange festive wishes. When I end the call I pass the phone to Bella and ask her to call her father.

Alan is spending Christmas with Mike. I feel incredibly guilty that our family is apart this year, and wonder how he is coping without the children today, it must be painful for him. He answers his phone immediately and he and Bella chat for a few minutes before she passes the phone to Joe.

Alan is obviously quizzing Joe to ascertain where we are, and who with, but Joe is far too keen to get on with present opening to talk for long and he thrusts the phone to me before running off to the great hall.

"Merry Christmas Alan," I say cheerily. "The kids are fine and having a great time." I can hear the hatred in his voice as he replies curtly, informing me that he has nothing to say to me other than he wishes to collect the children on the twenty seventh of December, which is typical of Alan. I had already agreed with him that Bella and Joe would be with me until New Year's Eve but there's little point antagonising him more. It means that I will have to curtail my wonderful break with Sebastian, but it really would anger Alan if he knew the children and I were here with another man. As far as Alan is concerned we are staying with Ruth for Christmas and I have already primed the children to back up that story, terrible though it is to make them lie. Not that it's any of Alan's concern but I want the divorce to go smoothly and uncontested. My life is stressful enough plus I want to avoid expensive lawyers' fees. Alan ends the call having gained agreement that I he will collect the children at four o'clock on the twenty-seventh.

Sebastian is clearly disappointed that we will be leaving early but we agree not to let it spoil a wonderful Christmas Day.

We open our presents by the fire in the morning room, where Joe has placed small piles of gifts and tells us where to sit, next to our respective present pile. It's such a beautiful room, with golden yellow silk walls and drapes of matching yellow silk, embroidered with Chinese flowers and birds. Small gold glitter reindeer thread along the mantel and a huge bowl of glitter encrusted fir cones stands by the fireside, with tiny twinkling white lights twisted around each cone.

Joe and Bella are delighted with their gifts. Sebastian gives Joe a remote controlled car, which is soon whizzing around the vast floors of the hallways. Bella unwraps an expensive new outfit by a London designer. Scarlett picked it out online, she tells Bella. *Don't let it wind you up, Beth*, I tell myself.

Sebastian places a long flat, red velvet box in my hands. Opening it slowly, I squeal with delight at the beautiful gold watch within.

"Sebastian!" I gasp. "It's too much."

"Nonsense," he replies. "Nothing is too much for my girl." He places the delicate timepiece on my left wrist and closes the clasp. It's an exquisite Cartier timepiece with a circlet of diamonds framing the dial. It must have cost a small fortune. He grins like a schoolboy, clearly delighted with my reaction to his generous gift.

"Thank you darling. I adore it and will wear it always." I kiss him hard on his mouth until the children cry "eww! Put him down."

Placing a small black box in his hand, I whisper "merry Christmas darling Sebastian." His eyes light up brighter than the Christmas tree and I picture him, here in this room as a boy on Christmas Day. I wonder if he was as happy then, as he seems now. Opening the box, he breathes "wow" as he slips the silver cufflinks into his palm.

"See the engraving?" I ask, pointing at the intricately turned letter engraved on each of the circular discs. "S and E. Do you see the tiny heart entwined under each of the letters?"

"I do, darling. Thank you, I will treasure them." We gross the children out again with our kisses.

Present opening complete, we feast on turkey and all the trimmings at the sumptuously laid table in the great hall, and Scarlett joins us, which perturbs me, but she's good company although laughing a little too raucously at Sebastian's jokes, and she chatting animatedly with Bella about fashion and music.

The afternoon is spent playing parlour games and it's refreshingly wonderful to see the children laughing. Sebastian is the perfect host and, later as we curl up in bed after midnight, I feel content.

"Have you had a good Christmas Mrs. Dove?" he asks.

"In the circumstances, yes thank you. It's been wonderful," I kiss his cheek.

"Are we ok?" he asks tentatively.

"We have a lot of issues to overcome, Sebastian. I don't want to spoil today though."

He strokes my hair. "Hey, I have another Christmas present for you."

"But you've given me the beautiful watch," I protest.

He reaches to the nightstand and pulls open the drawer, taking a small black velvet box tied with gold ribbon, and places it in my hand. Enthralled, I eagerly pull the ribbon and open the box. Inside is a breath-taking ring of platinum with two tiny hearts entwined, a sapphire at the centre of each heart, which are the palest blue like glacial ice. Sebastian takes it from the box and places it on the ring finger of my right hand.

"Sebastian, it's beautiful. We both gave each other hearts," I gasp.

"It's not a match for your beauty, darling. The blue of the sapphires is the palest and rarest - the colour of your eyes." Those blue eyes are filled with tears.

"This is the nicest thing anyone has ever done for me - the most precious gift, thank you."

"You are mine Elizabeth," he breathes. "Always mine and *only* mine."

"Yes, always yours. This means so much to me Sebastian." A tear rolls down my cheek, and Sebastian brushes it away with tenderly.

As I admire the beautiful ring, Sebastian moves the hair from my neck and plants feather light kisses from my earlobe to my shoulder. As tremors course through my body, I give myself to him completely.

It's time to leave and, with a heavy heart, I call the children while Sebastian puts our cases in the trunk.

He pulls me into his arms and we kiss deeply, passionately. I can feel hot tears prick my eyes and I don't want to go. I am going to miss Sebastian and Penmorrow – but I don't anticipate missing Scarlett, I do hate leaving them both alone together. A knot of pain forms in my stomach. "Don't cry Elizabeth. It's been truly wonderful having you and the children here. It feels as though you belong here... come back to me soon won't you?" he wipes my tears away and his eyes crinkle with an adoring smile.

I kiss him lightly and force a smile in return. "You won't be able to stop me! I've so loved being with you Sebastian... I miss you already!"

The children come running out of the house across the gravel driveway and Joe throws his arms around Sebastian who sweeps him up and spins him around before tussling his hair. "Hey big guy." Sebastian looks down at Joe. " You look after your old mum ok?"

"Not so much of the *old*," I protest.

Sebastian turns to Bella who seems to have really taken to him, which is rare for my moody teenage daughter.   He clutches her in a tight embrace and kisses her forehead affectionately and she blushes. "Bella Belle," he sighs tenderly. "Remember to watch that smart mouth of yours young lady and I hope to see you again really soon," he says.

"Yeh, whatever," she laughs and as she gets into the car she blows him a kiss and another for Scarlett who has joined Sebastian to say farewell.

"Drive safely darling," he tells me. "Call me when you get home and I'll try and drive up next week. Oh and happy New Year! I'm sure next year will be *your* year." He kisses me again and after hugging Scarlett, I get into the car and we set off down the tree-lined drive. I can see Scarlett and Sebastian waving and feel a twinge of jealousy at the closeness they share, the knot tightens in my stomach. I have a long journey ahead and enough time to dwell on this but also to consider how refreshingly different Sebastian is and how much I adore him already. Plus the sex is incredible; I had no idea what a whore I could be!

18

Bella is in a cantankerous mood today, adamant that she does not want to go to stay with Alan at Mike's house and I am losing patience with her.

"You *are* going and that's that!" I exclaim. "Remember, your father hasn't seen you since before Christmas and try and give some thought for others Bella instead of yourself."

"Get lost Mum. If he wasn't such a bloody loser he'd still be living here!" I slap her face. She catches her breath and puts her hand to her reddening cheek, her eyes brimming with hot tears.

"I *HATE* you," she screams as she runs out of the kitchen, taking the stairs two at a time. She slams her bedroom door behind her.

I switch on the kettle, still fuming but feeling guilty for striking her. I haven't hit her since she was three, and that was a tap on the back of her legs when she threw a terracotta flowerpot at me. She's always been feisty – takes after me, Alan always said.

Taking my steaming coffee into the lounge, I check Joe's bag again to make sure he has enough clothes for his stay with Alan. I call up to him to bring down his trainers and another pair of socks and hear one of the children running down the stairs. As I reach the door to the hallway I see Bella, coat on and bag slung over her shoulder, heading toward the front door. "Where the hell are you going?" I demand.

"I'm going to stay with Chloe from school. It's all arranged and you can't stop me. I've got my phone and money and I'll be back the day after tomorrow," and she slams out of the front door before I can protest or stop her. I throw open the door but she's sprinting up the road and disappears around the corner and I know I have to let her go. I text her immediately and tell her I am sorry for slapping her, I love her and ask her to text me when she gets to Chloe's house which I recall is only half a mile away. She doesn't reply.

Alan arrives thirty minutes late, and Joe is pacing the hall impatiently waiting for his father. Alan pushes past me and enters the house and I can smell whisky on his breath.

"Hello Alan. Did you have a nice Christmas?" I foolishly ask.

"Bloody great," he replies sarcastically. "C'mon Joe, get your bag son. Where's Bella?"

"She's gone off to stay with Chloe, sorry but you know how she can be. You... you've been drinking Alan. I don't think you should be driving, especially with Joe."

He looks contemptuously at me, although I notice his eyes don't focus on mine properly. How much has the man drunk? I feel panicky, sure now that I don't want Joe in a car with him while he is clearly smashed.

"Look, I'll make you a coffee. Stay and have a bite to eat and then leave a little later," I suggest. His face is full of loathing and his speech is a little slurred I notice.

"Typical, so you've poishoned my daughter now. Get in the car Joe, itsh unlocked. Beth you have no bloody right to tchell me what I can and fucking can't do so leave it…"

Joe looks from Alan to me and at Alan again, unsure which of his parents to obey. His brow creases as the volatility of the situation upsets him and his eyes brim with tears. He gauges his father's anger to be more acute and decides to do as his father says rather than antagonise him more, and he picks up his bag and reaches up to kiss me goodbye.

"Joe, put your bag down and go to your room. Everything's fine, your dad and I need to talk," I order. Joe puts his bag down and, red faced with tears tumbling down his cheeks, turns to go upstairs but Alan grabs his arm.

"GET IN THE CAR NOW" he barks. Alan picks up Joe's bag and I try to snatch it away from him. I'm overwhelmed with the sudden need to protect my son – mothers' instinct screaming through every cell of my body. Alan shoves my chest and I stumble back falling against the hard edge of the stair bannister knocking the wind out of me.

"Alan FOR GOD'S SAKE!" I scream but he seems like a different person; a man I don't know, not the man I've been married to for seventeen years. Joe is sobbing now and the next thirty seconds are a blur.

Alan pushes Joe through the open doorway and up the pathway, his bag clutched in Alan's hand. I see them but am powerless to stop them. My desolate boy, shoulders heaving as he cries, being jostled into the passenger seat of Alan's car and the screeching of tyres, as Alan speeds away. I'm sobbing too now, huge wracking sobs, which come from my core.

Hands shaking, I dial my mother's number and when she answers I can barely speak. I have a terrible dark foreboding, which I can't rationalise but my mother will understand. Only a mother can understand. My mother sooths me and tells me she is on her way to me.

Call twenty-seven. There's still no answer - just Alan's voicemail message.

Hi you've reached the voicemail of Alan Dove. I'm sorry I can't take your call but leave a message. Cheers.

I try Mike's mobile and landline numbers again and am about to hang up when he answers.

"Mike thank God," I sigh. "Look, Alan picked Joe up nearly two hours ago and he was drunk... and I know he's probably stopped off for something to eat... but I'm worried Mike. He was pissed again."

"He's not here Beth. Did you two fight?"

"Yes. But only because I wouldn't let him drive Joe when he'd been drinking. He reeked of booze Mike. Look, can you call me the minute they get there please?" I end the call.

My mother calls the accident and emergency department at the local hospital but thankfully, they've had no traffic accident victims admitted this evening. I try Bella's mobile number, wondering if Joe or Alan have been in touch with her but she curtly replies that she hasn't seen or heard from Alan and doesn't care if she never sees him again, 'the dick'. I waste no time admonishing her, instead I decide to drive to Mike's house in case Alan and Joe have arrived there. As I grab my coat from the hook by the front door my mobile phone rings, it is Mike.

"Beth love, there's been a terrible accident."

19

Mum holds my hand as we sit in the family room of the Accident and Emergency Department, at The Lakes General Hospital. It's a stark little room with peach walls, 1980's floral border and pastel striped curtains.

Mum and I sit together on the hard green sofa. A plastic cup of water has been thoughtfully placed on the battered old teak coffee table in front of me, next to the obligatory box of tissues and untactful leaflets on becoming an organ donor. I take a tissue from the box and blow my nose, my cheeks hot with fresh tears.

It's been forty minutes now and there is still no news of Alan and Joe. All we know so far is that Alan's car collided with a tree and it took the fire crew over an hour to cut Alan and Joe free, and paramedics a further twenty minutes to stabilise both prior to the journey to hospital. The emergency helicopter could not be diverted apparently due to it already attending a further accident near Dorchester. All this information serves to increase my sense of panic at the severity of their condition.

My phone pings and I look at the text message on the screen, it's Sebastian wondering why I haven't called him to say that I arrived home safely. I type a brief message back telling him about the accident, I will call him later. My phone immediately vibrates as Sebastian calls me and I stand and leave the room as I answer his call but a nurse shoots a disapproving look at me, so I exit through the automatic doors to the ambulance loading area and burst into tears when I hear Sebastian's voice.

He has such a soothing, calming tone as he assures me that the doctors will be doing all they can to help my boy and that he's sure that Joe will pull through, as he's such a tough little guy. Sebastian sounds genuinely concerned and choked up too and I am so grateful for his support, suddenly longing to feel his strong protective arms around me. Just listening to his comforting voice makes me feel calmer and he tells me he is on his way to me.

"Beth!" My mother bursts through the automatic doors and grabs my arm. "The doctor is looking for you, *come on!*" she implores.

I cut the call without saying goodbye, thrust the phone in to my coat pocket and follow mum back in to the family room where a tall, wiry doctor dressed in blue scrubs and rubbing the back of his neck is waiting for me. He tells me to sit down and I want to scream… "Joe?" my voice is thready, and barely audible.

"Mrs. Dove. Beth. My name is Doctor

David Sutherland. I'm the A&E registrar on duty, and I've been leading the team looking after your son and your husband. As you know, Joe and Alan were in a very bad way when they arrived here. Each had a Glasgow Coma Score of just three, Beth. This means that, in essence, their brains were not functioning. You must understand that they were both in the front seats of the car and both took the full force of the impact head on. I only say this so that you understand how difficult it has been to try and reverse the damage that was done. I have to tell you, Beth, with deep regret we have not been able to save either Joe or Alan."

My mother wails from somewhere in this cold miserable little room. I can't absorb what the doctor is saying to me. The room starts to spin and I hold on to my mother's arm to steady myself.

"Immediate CT scans showed considerable fracturing of the skull in Joe, and unfortunately Alan sustained a ruptured aorta on impact. I have to say, that neither will have been in any pain, nor have known anything about the accident. Mrs. Dove… Beth… I and my team are so very sorry for your loss."

My world falls apart.

Available now …
Sebastian
DARK BONDS
[Book two]

Elizabeth struggles to absorb tragic news that rocks her world. Her life seemingly in shreds, she is comforted by Sebastian through her darkest days. At his suggestion, she and daughter Bella stay at his ancient manor house, Penmorrow, for a period of healing; yet now Elizabeth must face not only the increasing sexual demands of the dominant Sebastian … but a darker undercurrent of malice. Who can she trust? A man who comforts yet controls her? Or his maid, Scarlett, who hints at her own dark past with her Lord.

Available now …
Sebastian
RETRIBUTION
[Book three]

When Elizabeth Dove met the dark, dominant Sebastian De Montfort, Lord of Penmorrow House in Cornwall, little did she know that tragedy would forever change her life. Now caught in a web of secrets, Elizabeth must fight a dark force within the ancient walls of Sebastian's manor house. Gripped by inexplicable madness, Elizabeth must endeavour to salvage her love as her dominant Lord demands her submission. Is she strong enough to survive?

Also, don't miss...
Sebastian's Journal

It is indeed a dark mind that feeds my soul. My recollections recorded herein, are written with no thought to their candour, for they serve only to exorcise ghosts and quench my sadistic thirst. My journal shall never be read, other than by my ancestors who will likely be as depraved as I. This knowledge affords me the freedom to write fact and fiction and to seamlessly blend the two within my short tales ... only I shall ever know the provenance of each.

My journal. My confidant. You judge me not for my dominant ways, nor seek retribution. Hold tight my secrets within your leather binding while I spill forth my prose and verse upon your chaste pages.

"Janey paints incredibly vivid and distinct characters – ones which evoke a strong emotional response. I must say, I think it's a mark of a talented author who can so effectively get inside my head."

[Review by christinahardingerotica.blogspot.co.uk]

ABOUT THE AUTHOR

Living on the south coast of England in a tranquil country setting, Janey leads a respectable life as mother to four fabulous children. Her days are spent as managing director of her own business, while she also dallies in politics. As darkness falls, so Janey loses herself to her true passion – writing. Surviving on four hours sleep each night, Janey burns the midnight oil letting her creativity loose … teasing from her mind the plethora of stories waiting to be told.

If you enjoyed this book, please do write a review here:

www.amazon.co.uk

www.goodreads.com

Please also follow me on Twitter:

@JaneyRosen

Why not visit my blog:

www.janeyrosen.me

Or my website:

www.janeyrosen.com

And like my Facebook page:

www.facebook.com/pages/Janey-Rosen

40365562R10179

Made in the USA
Charleston, SC
05 April 2015